THE MAN FROM YESTERDAY

THE MAN FROM YESTERDAY

SEYMOUR SHUBIN

ACADEMY CHICAGO PUBLISHERS

This novel is a work of fiction. Names, characters, places and incidents are either the product of the author's imagination, or, if real, used fictitiously.

Published in 2005 by
Academy Chicago Publishers
363 West Erie Street
Chicago, Illinois 60610

Printed in the U.S.A.

Library of Congress Cataloging-in-Publication Data
on file with the publisher

For Nathaniel Tae-Sun Shubin

NOVELS BY SEYMOUR SHUBIN

Anyone's My Name
Manta
Wellville, U.S.A.
The Captain
Holy Secrets
Voices
Never Quite Dead
Remember Me Always
Fury's Children
My Face Among Strangers
The Good and the Dead
A Matter of Fear

ONE

The Lieutenant—almost everyone still called him Lieutenant—was driving fast but with great caution, the way he used to in the old days when he was chasing a car: his main worry during those wild rides was always don't hurt anyone innocent, don't kill anyone innocent. And now he was driving with a little extra caution, because he didn't want anything to happen, not to him, not to anyone, before he got his message to the police.

Now and then he caught himself fantasizing that he was a cop again, working on this with his men; he had to yank himself back to reality. In fact, when he reached the Westend Detective District station house, which he had headed for twenty-one years, he automatically drove to the parking lot in back, only to be jolted by the sign at the entrance: POLICE ONLY. He stopped, suddenly just Jack Lehman again, and hesitated—the spot where that Ford was parked used to be his.

He saw a space on the street and reluctantly pulled into it.

He walked quickly to the building, at seventy-three no longer quite the six-footer he had been but still solidly built and holding himself with a certain dignity. His face was strong, without a mark from his boxing days, and his thin gray hair was carefully parted and brushed. Nothing about him revealed the nervousness that was spreading through him as he approached the door.

He hadn't been in this building since he retired, some fifteen years ago; he had hardly even driven past it, although he lived in the district. Just no reason to. And it wasn't as if he'd been pushed out. He had retired when his wife got sick and they had hoped that the Florida sun would help her. But beautiful little Trudy had died in Florida, and he moved back a month or two later to be with his son and grandchildren. Then, a couple of years later, he had met Ann. Like him, she was widowed.

As he walked in, he felt almost dizzy to see how little things had changed. The uniform boys of the 32nd District were still on the first floor, a separate world in a way, and up this short flight of steps was his old world, Westend. Everything seemed in its old place—offices, counters, hallways, open spaces, desks, bulletins on the walls. But most of all there was the feel of the place—the same, the same, and yet so strange.

On the second floor, a young detective in a sport shirt looked up from his desk.

"Can I help you, sir?"

"I'd like to talk to whoever's in charge." It was some new guy, he'd heard; he hadn't taken the time to find out his name.

"That's Captain Hewitt. He's busy now. Can I help you?"

"I'm Jack Lehman. I used to be commander here. I've got something important, very important."

"Oh?" The young man's eyes widened, and he stood up. He held out his hand and the Lieutenant took it. "Good to meet you, sir. Let me see what the captain's doing."

A couple of minutes later he brought him to the captain's office. The first thing that struck the Lieutenant as he walked in was how this had changed. It was a modern office now, with a fancy mahogany desk and leather chairs. His own desk had been a green metal job, and on his wooden chair he used a seat cushion he'd brought from home.

The captain, a man in his late thirties, a little shorter than the Lieutenant, got up and came around his desk to shake hands. The captain had recently replaced the commander who had replaced the Lieutenant. "It's good to meet you. I've heard a lot about you."

"Thanks. Look, I don't want to take up much of your time, but I want to pass along something I've learned. It's about a big heist. A tremendous heist. Like over a million dollars."

"Oh?" The captain frowned.

"A guy called me. Used to be one of my sources. Very reliable. Very."

The Lieutenant took a deep breath. He didn't know why he was still so nervous; he was furious at himself.

Captain Hewitt sensed this and tried to help. "Is this something that's going to happen?"

The Lieutenant shook his head. "No, it already happened. And my source told me who was hit."

"You have the name?"

"Yeah, he gave it to me. Told me on the phone. It's someone named . . ."

But suddenly he couldn't remember. Frozen, he looked at the captain helplessly, and slowly brought his hand to his left temple. Oh God! He began racing through the alphabet for help. Did it begin with an S? No, not an S. L? F?

Captain Hewitt asked quietly, "Did you happen to write it down?"

No, I didn't write it down! Like a stupid ass, I didn't write it down! L? Was it an L?

The captain was looking at him. "But you know who told you."

Even that—he couldn't remember even that! Just that the guy had a nickname he used to know like his own name.

"Why don't you just sit down and try to relax? It'll come to you."

No, no, no! It was lost!

"Let me just ask you this," the captain said. "How long ago was this heist?"

Oh God! "Not long ago. But I don't know." Even—he could tell, he could hear it—even his voice suddenly sounded frail.

"I mean, a job that big. You'd think we'd have heard . . ."

He looked at the captain. "I—I'll think, let me think. I—I'll get back to you."

"Sure. Just take it easy."

"I'll get back to you," he repeated.

He turned and walked out of the office, down the corridor, using the handrail on the stairs. It was only when he was out on the sidewalk that the burning in his eyes turned into tears.

TWO

THE CALL HAD COME this morning after the most frightening night of his life, more frightening than any fifty bad times he'd ever had on the force.

He had been lying in bed watching TV with his wife Ann, and, as on many other nights, he had fallen asleep without realizing that he was becoming sleepy. He woke with a kind of jolt, to daylight and voices—only it wasn't daylight, it was the brightness of the screen, and the voices came from the images there. He stared at one of the two people on the screen, a man at a desk, the host of the show, and several minutes later was still struggling to think of his name.

He shouldn't have tried to think of it right then, when he was still groggy. It was stupid to try, but now he was stuck with it, and his concern was beginning to build into panic.

God, he knew that name as well as he knew his own. He watched him just about every night, except once in a while he watched that other guy, what was his name—Leno, Jay Leno! A surge of relief went through him that at least this had come to him, and he told himself to let it go at that, to just watch the program, but—it was like this guy, this star he watched just about every night, this guy everyone in the whole world knew, had no name at all.

It was like, How can he have a name when I can't think of it?

It was really like that, like he had absolutely no name.

He wanted to turn to Ann and say, "Who is it? Tell me who it is." It would be so easy to say that, but he had to think it out on his own, he had to smash through this wall in his head. Anyway, he'd been asking her questions like that often lately, and she was beginning to get irritated with him, because she couldn't seem to get through to him what she kept saying each time: "Everyone has that when they get a little older. You think I remember everything?"

That was at least some attempt to make him feel better, not like Peter's reaction. The few times his son came over, and even when the kids were around and they were all having fun, it seemed like half the time Peter was looking to see if his old man had lost his marbles. It was like he was looking for a reason to send him to a nursing home.

Jack got up to go to the bathroom. When he came back Ann said, "You missed something so funny I can't explain."

He turned on his side, his back to her. He told himself that this wasn't the first time this had happened, and that sooner or later the name would come to him, mostly when he wasn't trying to think of it. Usually he woke up in the middle of the night, and God, there it was, so clear you could only wonder how you could have forgotten it.

All he had to do was just relax. Why was he letting himself get so panicky this time?

He lay on his left side, his hand resting on his right shoulder, the way he remembered his father slept. His father had not lived long enough to go through this.

He had to stop scaring himself.

Then he thought of something that seemed so unbelievable now, so cruel, so unthinking that it made him cringe. He remembered—when was this? Only nine, ten years ago, when Trudy was still alive, God rest her soul—he remembered a party at their house and everyone laughing at this story of Trudy's cousin's husband, a famous surgeon who started losing it and one day turned to his wife and said, "Mary, when did I start to go flooey?"

Oh, how they had all laughed!

This guy who used to take apart knees and shoulders and had invented so many surgical tools, devices.

The Lieutenant kept thinking of that surgeon, as though all this was a kind of punishment. And then slowly, against his will, he tried to remember the surgeon's name. Roy? It wasn't Roy, but something close to it. The last name, he couldn't even begin to think of his last name, but he was sure—and this was so aggravating, he was so close to it—he was sure his first name began with an R.

A few hours later, when he woke from an unexpected sleep, he couldn't believe he'd thought it began with an R. It was Gordon. Gordon Crane. Of course! It was so clear.

And that other guy, that star—

Letterman. Oh Christ. David Let-ter-man.

He lay there, breathing heavily through his mouth, listening to the comforting thumps of his heart.

It was as if his whole head had opened up and bright clear spring water was running over him. He wanted to bathe his whole being in it, to let it flow through him. Afterward he slept through the rest of the night, waking a little after nine, which was unusually late for him. He woke to the clatter of dishes in the kitchen of their one-bedroom apartment, and the smell of coffee. He had sat on the side of the bed, still a little sleepy, and feeling as if he'd spent been the night wrestling with someone.

He was starting to get dressed when the phone rang.

"I'll take it," Ann had called from the kitchen. Then, moments later, "Jack, it's for you."

"Who is it?"

"I don't know. Should I find out?"

"Never mind."

He sat back on the bed and picked up the receiver from the night table.

"Yes?"

"Lieutenant." The voice, a man's, was soft, almost a whisper. "How are you, it's me," and he had identified himself. "But I gotta talk fast."

"I can't hear you. I can hardly hear you."

"Lieutenant, I gotta talk fast. I'll tell you more later. But you know me, you know you can trust me. You always could. And there's no one I trust more'n you, that's why I'm callin'."

The voice had described the crime and given the name of the victim. It was so simple that the Lieutenant didn't think he needed to write it down.

Or maybe, he thought now as he sat in torment in his car outside the station house, he had simply forgotten to write it down.

THREE

HE HIT HIS FIST against the steering wheel. He hit it again. He wanted to turn on the ignition and drive away fast, away from this place and the captain's sudden, awful look of pity. But he mustn't! He was going to sit here until he remembered those names.

But then there were Hewitt's words.

"A job that big, you'd think we'd have heard . . ."

That was true—unless, say, it wasn't discovered yet. Or it was in another country. Or a million other things.

The guy on the phone never did say where it happened or who was behind it—just who had been ripped off. But maybe even more important, though the Lieutenant couldn't remember the informant's name, he knew as well as he knew his own face that that informant was someone who had helped him long ago on some important busts.

But who? Who was it?

It was maddening.

One of the problems was that there were so many informants, so many guys—mostly guys—he'd cultivated over the years. He'd never taken a crooked dime in his life, not one cent, but he'd helped so many guys get out on parole, and there were all those Halloween and Christmas parties for the kids. His district had been mostly a poor area during those years, with more than its share of drugs and violent crime, but sections of it had become gentrified: many of the old houses were remodeled or replaced and there were new apartment buildings like the one he lived in now.

The thing was, he shouldn't have trouble remembering old names. New ones were what gave him problems, and then only once in a while. But old names? Hardly ever. There was—he began picking names at random—old Miss Bracken way way back in kindergarten, and that fat lady teacher—Moblin—in third or fourth grade. And every crime he'd ever handled! That poor Poletski girl, strangled in the woods—Joan, Joan Poletski—and old Albert Cramer, shot dead in his grocery store, and that son-of-a-bitch rapist, Colletti—he almost beat him to death after a long chase on foot.

Shouldn't have trouble with anything back there at all. None. Hardly anything, anyway.

He tried to calm down, and not think of that look on the captain's face. But it was so hard not to. And with his heart thumping like that.

And then, one word came to him.

Monsoon.

His informant's name wasn't Monsoon, but it was something like it. Munson . . . Muncie . . . Monty . . . He still didn't have the name, but now he could visualize the guy's face. A short fellow, black hair, who'd served lots of short time. And was grateful to him.

He sat up, turned on the ignition and drove off.

He started to pull over to a pay phone but changed his mind. He didn't want to bother going through a phone book or asking pain-in-the-ass Information—he knew where Tom lived. He and Ann had been there for dinner just a couple of months ago. Tom had been the first guy at the district to congratulate him when he'd taken over, a stranger there. There'd been a lot of resentment at the time; he'd felt it for months. Not only had one of their own been passed over, but here was this guy, a Jew!

Nearing Tom's place, he began to feel a growing excitement, a feeling different from his nervousness at the station. He felt as if he were back with his sergeant working on a case again.

He realized he should have called first, when he saw the look on Peggy's face as she opened the door. She was in a decent housecoat, but she suddenly clutched it at the throat.

"Sorry, Peggy," he said. "I was in the neighborhood."

"That's all right, Lieutenant, that's fine."

"Is Tom home?"

"Yes. He's upstairs. Yes. Come in, please come in."

Tom was halfway down the steps, looking on curiously, as the Lieutenant came into the living room. He said, grinning, "Hey. Lieutenant."

It was still always Lieutenant and Sarge. The warmth that came from fighting many wars together.

"Hey, good to see you." Tom stuck out a large hand. He was a few years younger than the Lieutenant, short and stocky, his hair cropped the way it had always been, though all white now.

Sitting on the sofa with Tom, the Lieutenant tried to think where to begin. He didn't want to say anything heavy about his memory, his nervousness about it. Maybe better to say nothing at all about it, to work around it.

"Look, Sarge, I got this call yesterday." He went into it, saying that the informant had given him his own name but not the name of the victim. "He sort of mumbled it and hung up. It sounded like Monsoon or Munson or Muncie. Something like that. And I'm just wondering if that might ring some kind of bell with you."

Tom looked at him thoughtfully. Then he sat back and pulled at his lips. He leaned forward again, resting his elbows on his knees.

"No." He shook his head. "Can't think of anyone."

"I connect him with a guy, a short guy with black hair who was a pretty lousy burglar, but he did a lot of them."

"A burglar," Tom repeated. "Huh." Then, "Did he say anything about where he's living now?"

"No, it was only when he hung up I realized he didn't."

"Huh. And you took it to the district."

"Yeah." But he said nothing about what had happened there.

Tom sat up a little and looked at him. "Over a million, you say."

"That's what he said."

"And the district never heard anything about a haul like that."

"Right."

"I know I haven't. I mean, I read newspapers. And I listen to TV. And my daughter's even got me on the Internet."

"It could be an out-of-town job."

"Still, that's a mighty big haul, Lieutenant."

"Or out of the country. Or maybe no one's missed the money yet."

"Over a million?" Tom looked at him quizzically. "Lieutenant, seriously. No offense. How do you know the guy's not a joker?"

"Because I connect him with a guy who never bullshitted me."

"Huh. Look," he said after some thought, "we're just talking. I'm not questioning anything but we're just talking. But you must have tried to get him to repeat his name. I mean, you say he was mumbling, half-whispering."

"Of course I tried."

"He wouldn't do it? Or you still just couldn't catch it?"

"Sarge, I tried. I said I tried."

"Oh, I didn't mean you didn't. I was just saying."

"Of course I tried."

"Hey, you sound sore. Please don't get sore at me. I was just wondering why the guy wouldn't speak up."

"I'm not sore at you, Tom. I'm just telling you what happened."

"I know. And I'm just . . . you know, asking questions."

"Sure." He just wanted to get out of there now.

"Let me give it some thought. Right now I can't come up with anything. But maybe something will come to me."

"Sure." The Lieutenant stood up, and now Tom got up too.

"Lieutenant, how about something to eat?"

"No, nothing. Thanks."

"Something to drink?"

"No, nothing."

"Well, tell me. How are things in general?"

"Fine. Couldn't be better. You?"

"Good. Great. Well . . . you take it easy, Lieutenant."

Like, the Lieutenant was thinking, don't go senile. He held out his hand. "See you, buddy."

"You take it easy," Tom said again. Then, at the door, "Watch those steps."

The Lieutenant deliberately walked down keeping away from the railing.

FOUR

DRIVING OFF, HE TRIED not to be annoyed at Tom. They'd been friends for too long, had been through too much together. But all he wanted was to be believed. His head might not be working completely the way it used to, but there was enough left that he knew what he knew, what he felt. It was like when he would call out something like, "There's a guy behind that wall with a gun!" Damn it, they knew there was a guy behind that wall with a gun. So they should believe him now, trust his instincts!

The sight of his apartment building didn't help. He didn't hate the place, but he hadn't really liked it from the day they moved in. Everyone knew everyone's business: So-and-So is getting a divorce, So-and-So's son is a fairy, didn't you know? And if you didn't say hello the right way in the lobby, someone was sure to ask you or Ann later that day if you were really okay. His rowhouse, even though it was in the middle of the block, had been nowhere as bad. That house seemed crushed on both sides by neighbors, and in a way even by those across the narrow street, but somehow there was a kind of large space between you and the others. A big part of it, maybe, was respect. That was the neighborhood where they'd seen him come up from motorcycle cop to detective to head of a district. They were proud of him, but they knew he was one of them. Here in this condo he was living among millionaires, where an ex-cop was sort of a curiosity.

And that was another thing. Their small apartment. Ann had had her heart set on this building, even though they could only afford a one-bedroom, one-bath apartment there. He'd wanted a den, at least, or some kind of workroom. When he lived in the house, he used to do a lot of wood work. And for the past year or so, he'd been doing volunteer work at one of the hospitals, two days a week, mostly pushing patients in wheelchairs. But they came up with too many volunteers and it was boring just standing around.

* * *

He sensed the instant he walked in that Ann wasn't home. Could be she was out at the pool behind the building. He put on shorts, a T-shirt and sneakers, and went down to the gym in the basement. It was empty: everyone was outside. He used the treadmill for almost half an hour, working up a good sweat, then went to his locker and changed into swim trunks. He didn't feel like going outside; wasn't up to talking to anyone. There was a small pool without a diving board in the gym. He dove into the deep end, and after about ten long strokes was at the other end, and turning. He'd loved swimming from the time he was a kid, was always at the Y when he wasn't working after school. He swam easily now, not wanting to think or feel. After about seventy-five laps, he floated on his back, propelling himself gently with his feet.

Then, while he was thinking of almost nothing, he remembered that stories about two of his old investigations had been published a few months earlier in a couple of true-detective magazines. He was sure the informant was named in one of them.

* * *

In the apartment, he went directly to the hall closet, where he knew he had put both magazines on the top shelf. The closet was neat as usual—Ann was a demon housekeeper—filled mostly with their outdoor clothes. There were some hats on the shelf along with a couple of manila envelopes holding newspaper clippings about him—arrests, awards, talks to community organizations; he'd thrown a lot of them away before he went to Florida. He lifted everything up, but the magazines were not there.

He stared in disbelief.

There was a two-drawer cardboard filing cabinet in one corner. He ran his hand across the top of the cabinet, then, on his knees, searched under the hanging garments. Nothing. He went into the bedroom and looked in Ann's closet. He pulled open his drawers, one at a time. He looked in the bathroom, though he knew that was totally crazy, and in the broom closet. Then he went back to the hall closet and stood before the open door.

He turned when he heard his wife come in.

"Ann?"

"Yes?" She was in her robe, from the pool. A tall slender woman in her late sixties, with short gray hair, she was from an old Quaker family and the widow of an assistant D.A.

"Ann, I had two magazines here. Right up there, on the shelf. Did you see them?"

"No," she answered after a moment, frowning.

"You know which magazines I mean. Those detective story things? I showed them to you."

"Yes," she answered slowly, "I remember. Of course."

"Where are they? I put them up there."

"I don't know, Jack. How would I know?"

"Well, they were up there and I never moved them."

"Well, I never moved them either."

"Well, somebody moved them."

"Jack, we don't have a maid. And I never touched them. Maybe"—she hesitated—"maybe you just forgot."

He felt a surge of anger. But he held back. The rare times he'd ever lost his temper with Ann, he'd always regretted it. How could he be angry at someone who was such a good person, who obviously cared for him? But his thoughts raced back to Trudy, to that early marriage without premarital agreements. They were both Jewish, but their backgrounds had been so different that he wondered sometimes how he had gotten her to marry him.

Her father was an osteopath and she was a college graduate and a social worker. The Lieutenant came from a poor family, where he was the oldest of three children and had to provide support starting in high school after his father died. He'd tried boxing before serving as an Army M.P. for a couple of years, which led to his joining the police force. Trudy's family was not delighted with her choice of a husband.

He became aware that the phone was ringing. He decided to let Ann answer; he didn't feel like talking to anyone. But the phone kept ringing.

He got up and lifted the receiver on the kitchen wall.

"Yes."

"Dad," his son said, "it's me. How are you?"

"Okay. I'm all right."

A pause. Then Peter said, cautiously, "What's wrong? You don't sound good."

"Nothing's wrong. I'm fine."

"Dad, let me ask you something. When's the last time you saw the doctor?"

Alarmed, suddenly he was sure Ann had told Peter he was having problems with his memory, that she was more worried about him than she let on. "I don't know. Not long ago."

"How long?"

"I don't know. Four months. I don't know."

"Come on, Dad, it's been longer than that. A lot longer."

"I don't know."

"Dad, I want you to call him. Get a checkup. Tell him . . ." But he didn't finish.

"I'll see. But I feel fine."

"Look . . ." Another pause, a long one. "Look, I'll stop over in the morning. I want to talk to you."

"Why?"

"What do you mean why? I want to talk to you. I want to see you."

"I'm fine, I'm telling you."

"Can't I see you? Don't you want to see me?"

He didn't answer, didn't know what to say.

"So you take it easy. And I'll see you tomorrow."

Slowly the Lieutenant hung up the phone, and stood feeling helpless. He knew what his son wanted the doctor to do: probe his head, not his body. Who is this, who is that, what is this, do you remember . . . ? But who in hell wouldn't forget things, sitting across from a doctor who held what was left of your life in his hands?

And Peter was coming over. He could come in the morning and not have to hurry to work, because he was an architect and worked at his own speed. Never in his life had the Lieutenant thought that he would someday want to hide from his own son, to run away from him.

FIVE

ANN WENT TO BED early. He sat alone in the living room, trying to lose himself in television. But he kept switching from channel to channel and finally turned it off. His mind kept going back to that voice on the phone, telling him about a crime that no one else had heard of. Out there somewhere in a foggy swirl was his one tiny chance to be found normal, to be normal. How could he find out who that voice belonged to? That detective magazine was his only hope, but he couldn't even remember what it was called, let alone the name of the writer. All he could remember about him was that he was fairly young and lived somewhere over a store. The guy had contacted him, saying there were these two cases of his he'd like to write up; so the Lieutenant had gone to see him and they'd had a good conversation. And over the next few months he'd gotten copies of the magazines. Those damn magazines.

But what was the writer's name?

A few minutes later, frowning, he was slowly getting to his feet. The bedroom door was still closed. He turned on the light, and quietly opened the door to the hall closet.

He had remembered that the fellow had contacted him initially by mail. But even if he'd filed the letter away, he had no idea what it was filed under. He opened the top drawer of the filing cabinet very slowly, afraid that the slightest sound would wake Ann. Only a handful of files held anything, since he'd thrown most of his old letters away when he left for Florida. Kneeling on one knee he began pulling out the few files that contained letters. Nothing leaped out at him. At the back of the bottom drawer was a small Beretta 25 and a box of cartridges. He hadn't bought his service revolver when he retired, something he soon regretted, so he bought this one. But where Trudy had accepted guns without liking them, Ann hated them and insisted on this piece being packed away. He wouldn't live without a gun.

He remained kneeling there, thumbing through the files. Then he opened the top drawer again, making himself go slower as he started once more with the A's. Then, under N, he lifted out the one file that held a letter. He looked at it, started to put it back, then stood up to look at it more carefully under the light.

Dear Mr. Lehman:

I am a free-lance writer (three nonfiction books and many magazine articles) with a special interest in crime . . .

It was signed Colin Ryan.

* * *

He woke a little before seven. Careful not to wake Ann, he slipped out of bed, gathered up his clothes and took them into the living room, where he dressed quietly. Luckily she apparently was not disturbed by water noises in the bathroom.

In the kitchen he looked at the letter again. He was eager to call Ryan, but it was far too early. Then there was the worry that Peter was stopping by on the way to his office. He could picture Peter trying not to show concern, but asking him question after question, actually grilling him, and then he himself losing his temper and raising his voice, making everything worse.

He had to hold Peter off.

He wouldn't be able to do it forever, but he couldn't think beyond today, beyond a day at a time.

He folded the letter, put it in his pocket, reached for the small pad of paper next to the phone and printed:

HAVE SOMETHING TO DO . BACK LATER.

* * *

He walked in the already-hot July sun the short distance to the building's parking lot and drove a few blocks to a 7-Eleven; he drank coffee in his car. The first time he glanced at his watch it was twenty after eight. The next, almost ten of nine. It was still early, but he walked to the public phone, holding the letter in his hand.

"Hello?"

"Is this Mr. Ryan?"

"That's right. Who's this?"

"This is Jack Lehman. The retired cop?"

"Oh, of course. Lieutenant. How are you, Lieutenant?"

"Okay. I'm okay. I know it's early but I hope you don't mind me calling. I was just wondering. Those two magazines, I wonder if you have them."

"You mean the ones with your cases?"

"Yes."

"Sure, I have them. But didn't the magazine send you copies?"

"Yeah, but I don't know what happened to them."

"Well, I've got copies. You want me to mail them to you?"

"I was wondering, could I just look at them? I want to see something."

"Certainly. Of course. You want to come over?"

"If it's okay."

"Sure. When would you like?"

"Now?"

"Now'll be fine."

Back in the car he looked at the address on the letterhead. He thought to himself that although he might forget the name of a guy he had met just ten seconds ago, he had a map of the city fixed firmly in his head. He'd driven on just about every one of those streets; first as a motorcycle cop and then as a detective, and not only driven on them but raced through a lot of them, watching not only the speeding car ahead but also cars at intersections, and the people frozen at the curbs.

Colin Ryan lived on a small street dotted with antique shops and art galleries. He shook the Lieutenant's hand warmly. "It's good to see you. How about a cup of coffee?"

The apartment, above a frame store, was handsome and filled with books. Ryan was in his early thirties, tall in spite of a slight stoop, and with an unruly mop of black hair falling loosely over his forehead. He'd dropped out of law school after the first year, more interested in writing about crime than in defending criminals. Occasionally he wrote for detective magazines under a pen name.

"No," the Lieutenant answered. "I've just had some. Thanks."

"Well, look, I've got the magazines right here."

Ryan, perhaps sensing the Lieutenant's tension, picked them up from his desk and handed them to him. The magazine, *Crime Central*, had lurid splashy covers featuring bosomy women cowering from danger, and featured one old investigation each month. The Lieutenant sat on the sofa with the two copies. One story was titled "The Jabbering Dead Man," the other, "Five Roads to a Cell." Both crimes had taken place in the seventies. He began going through the stories slowly, not really reading them but stopping his forefinger at every name. In "Five Roads to a Cell," he recognized the name of the informant. Phil Mondisi.

He had been one of the Cool Head Gang, five young punks who terrorized the city with a series of holdups and arsons. They'd all gotten fifteen to forty years, but of course eventually got out on parole, and Mondisi's time was cut when he acted as a prison snitch. After that he became one of the Lieutenant's "ears."

But what was his nickname, the one everyone knew him by and which he'd used on the phone?

The Lieutenant looked over at Colin Ryan, sitting behind his desk. "Can I use your phone book?"

"Of course."

The Lieutenant went through it, standing up. No Mondisi. He took a small notebook out of his pocket and carefully printed: PHIL MONDISI.

"You know," Ryan said, "you can have the magazines if you want them."

"Sure. Thanks."

"That's okay. And if there's anything else I can do for you, just let me know." At the door, he said, "It was a real pleasure working with you. And maybe we can do more of your old cases some day."

"Whenever you'd like."

"Take care of yourself," Ryan added, with a touch of concern.

SIX

HE DROVE OFF, THE magazines on the seat next to him, the air conditioner on. He had hoped he would get a new address for Mondisi but he did remember where the fellow used to live, in a rooming house in the district. The thing was, that was about fifteen years ago.

Now and then he caught himself speeding and slowed up sharply. That's all he needed, a ticket. But soon he was driving slowly, looking for 43rd Street. Glancing at the street signs he watched the numbers rise—37, 38 . . . It was weird, he thought: You can forget your own phone number but you remember that Mondisi had lived on 43rd Street, a street of gray-stone rowhouses, storefronts and bars. He drove for three blocks, all of them pretty much the same, before pulling over to the curb when the rowhouses became brick. He had hoped that somehow he would recognize the place, but the only thing he was reasonably sure of was that it was a stone house. He stepped out of the car into the golden heat. And into the past.

Squinting in the sun, he walked back to the stone houses. He had forgotten his sunglasses. There was so much going on in his head. Over there was the house where he'd carried a missing kid up the steps to his weeping parents. And that apartment over there—well, it wasn't that one but it was one like it—was where they finally ended a hostage situation, the hostage being the guy's wife with a gun to her head.

All these streets held something for him—happy, sad and in-between. Some of the guys he grew up with, who became lawyers or doctors or just plain rich, used to ask why he didn't start his own agency; and there had been times when—he hated to admit this even to himself—he had felt touches of envy. But these streets were where he belonged, this was what he was meant to do. Even his mother, after his first few weeks on a motorcycle, pretty much conceded it—"Just don't get hoit." And it was funny how those same old friends came to look on him with a certain pride, had him over to speak at their synagogues and churches and Rotaries.

He kept looking at the houses on both sides of the street.

He just couldn't tell, couldn't tell.

"Lieutenant."

He turned: an elderly woman was standing at the bottom of her steps, smiling and waving at him. She walked over, a stocky Italian woman with a lined kindly face. She reached out and clasped his hands with both of hers.

"I wasn't sure," she said. "I couldn't believe it. But you know something? You haven't changed that much. Oh, it's so good to see you, Lieutenant."

"It's good seeing you."

"Grayer. Whiter. A little thinner maybe. But I'd recognize you anywhere."

"I'm glad to see you again too." But God, what was her name?

"I want you to know something else. I will never forget. Never. I'll always be grateful."

But he didn't remember.

Walking on, he was still searching his memory, but then he was distracted by the hunt for the house. There were certain differences between some of them—an aluminum awning perhaps, window blinds instead of shades, an urn or a little statue on the top step. But nothing that grabbed at him. When he found himself at the end of the last block of stone houses, he turned back. His tension building, he walked a little faster, glancing at each side of the street. Finally desperate, he walked up the steps of a house and rang the bell. The door was opened partway by a man of about sixty.

"Pardon me, sir, but I'm looking for someone and I wonder if you could help me. He used to live around here years ago. Name of Philip Mondisi. Mondisi."

The man stared at him.

"He has a nickname," the Lieutenant continued. "And maybe you know him by that. I'm not sure of it exactly, but it's—like Muncie or Mooney."

"No." Abruptly. The door closed.

He tried another house at random. The woman who answered was polite, but she couldn't remember hearing of any Mondisi. It was the same at two bars, and several stores. But at a hoagie shop around the corner, the owner said cautiously, "Why do you want to know?"

"I haven't seen him in a long time. And it's important I reach him."

The man kept looking at him as if trying to read who he was; had to be thinking something like He's too old to be a cop, too old to be a bill collector or anything else bad. But he said, "I just can't give it out like that. Let me call him. I'll put you on, okay?"

"Sure. I appreciate it."

He went into the back of the store and returned holding a piece of paper which he consulted as he picked up the phone. But apparently the line was busy, and it stayed busy through several more tries. Then after staring searchingly at the Lieutenant once more, he printed something on the paper and slid it wordlessly across the counter to him. An address.

Outside, the Lieutenant began walking quickly. After a block or so, he began to notice that things looked strange, as if he had magically entered a different part of the city. He stopped and stood there, unable to believe he was lost in this district. In his own district.

He turned and started to walk back. But this felt wrong too—until half a block down he saw the sign of a hair salon. And he remembered parking in front of it.

* * *

The address, some six blocks away, was in a block of old semi-detached houses with open front porches. He sat in his car, looking at the house, trying to ignore what he couldn't ignore, that the long walk in the heat after a terrible night had tired him. He walked up to the porch and rang the bell. The door opened within seconds, almost flew open, and the fortyish woman, her blond hair in disarray, looked wide-eyed with anticipation. But that look faded quickly.

"Oh," she said. "Oh." Then, desperately, "Who are you? What do you want?"

"I'm looking for Mr. Mondisi. Are you his wife?"

"Yes. No." She shook her head in confusion. "I—I'm sorry. He lives here, we live together. Who are you?"

"An old friend of his. My name's Lehman. Jack Lehman."

She stared at him. Then, slowly, "You're a policeman, aren't you?"

"I was, yes."

"Yes," she repeated. She seemed almost dazed. "I remember Moogie mentioning you. He thought you were a great guy."

Moogie—Moogie, of course! "Well, we were friends. I haven't seen him in years . . . Does he happen to be home?"

"That's it, that's why I'm going crazy. He should have been home last night. He left yesterday right after lunch and I haven't seen him since. I'm going crazy!"

She opened the door wider and stepped back. The Lieutenant followed her in, suddenly energized. Moogie missing? After he made that call?

He asked her, "Do you know where he was going?"

"Sure. He said he was going to see a friend, an old friend, Stan Sherry. Stan's in a rehab hospital, he broke his hip. Moogie was going to spend the afternoon with him. But I called Stan and Moogie never went there."

"Did Moogie ever do this before?"

"You mean just not show up?" She shook her head, but then added, "Oh, a couple years ago, he did that once or twice. But he was drinking then. He's been off it at least a year and a half, maybe two."

"What's the longest he was gone?"

"Just one night. But like I said, he was drinking then."

"Let me ask you this. How's he been? Has he seemed worried about anything? Upset?"

"No, I don't think so. I mean, I know so. I mean, if he was he never said."

The Lieutenant wondered whether he should tell her anything about Moogie's call. It was the kind of confidence he'd never broken in his life, but he said, "He called me yesterday morning. Do you know anything about it?"

She stared at him, puzzled. "He called you? No."

"He said he had something he wanted to talk to me about. You have any idea what it could be?"

"No." She shook her head.

"Do you know if he got himself involved in something?"

"You mean illegal? Oh no! I'll swear to that. Honest to God."

"Did he ever say anything about anyone else being involved in something?"

"You mean doing something crooked? No."

"Have you told the police he's missing?"

"Yes, I called them this morning. But it was like . . . so what, call 'em back in a few days if he still didn't show up."

"And there was no problem between you two?"

"Oh no, no. Not at all. He—he was even talking about us getting married. And that was something he never talked about, we never talked about. And it just came out."

"Has he been working?"

She shook her head. "No, he hurt his back. He was doing pick ups for a dry cleaner and he hurt his back bad. He's been on disability."

About fifteen minutes later he was back sitting in his parked car. The woman, Helene Castle, had given him the name of the rehab center where Stan Sherry was staying, as well as the names and addresses of a few of Moogie's other friends. Moogie could be sleeping off a drunk somewhere. Still, he had disappeared after making that call—was that a coincidence?

He became aware after a few moments that he was staring at the magazines he'd put on the seat. He picked up the top one and turned to "Five Roads to a Cell," with its old photos of him—his hair black—and some of his boys, half of them now dead, standing with Moogie and his four buddies at a crime scene or a hearing. There had been a time when he had assumed, without thinking about it, that he would remember those guys' names forever; that he would remember everything forever. Now he was skimming the story again, stopping to print their names in his notebook.

Joe Lippen. Chris Quint. Emil Dalenski and his younger brother Mike.

He went up to the house again, this time to ask Helene if she knew if Moogie was still friendly with any of them. But after studying the names closely, she said no.

* * *

The Baumann Rehabilitation Center was about ten miles away, on the northern edge of the city. The Lieutenant had no trouble finding it: he'd visited many people there over the years, going back to his motorcycle days. The receptionist gave him a room number and told him how to find it.

Stan Sherry was in his room, sitting in a wheelchair in street clothes, watching TV intently. He looked to be about fifty, a few years older than Moogie. He turned as if sensing the Lieutenant's presence.

"If you're looking for my roommate he's in the lounge."

"No, I hope you don't mind, I'd appreciate a word with you."

Sherry looked at him. "Who're you?"

"Jack Lehman. I'm a friend of Phil Mondisi's. Moogie."

Quickly: "They hear from him?"

"No. I just came from his house. I was talking to his ladyfriend. She told me he was supposed to see you yesterday."

Sherry's face sagged. "Damn it, damn it. Now tell me again, who're you?"

"Like I said, I'm a friend, an old friend. I'm a retired detective lieutenant."

"And Helene sent you over."

"That's right."

Sherry frowned. "I don't know where the hell that guy could be. He said he'd be here yesterday at one o'clock. Did you see him at one? I didn't. I'm scared for him. This don't make sense."

"Helene said he used to do this once in a while a couple years ago."

"Really? Oh. When he was drinkin'. He hasn't been drinkin'. I'm tellin' you, I know. He'd tell me. We've been buddies a long time, which is unusual when a guy's working for you."

"You own the dry cleaning place?"

"Oh, you know that. And I guess you know he got hurt. A guy plowed into his van, a kid. And he really got hurt. He never faked nothin'. I know."

"Am I right in thinking you've been talking to him lately? I mean that he just didn't call you out of the blue?"

"That's right."

"How's he seemed to you lately? Worried? Has he been acting different in any way?"

Sherry paused for moment. "You know, I think so. I haven't seen him since my operation—I had a new knee put in—but we were talkin' almost every day. And the past couple days, I thought he sounded a little jumpy."

"What made you think that?"

"I don't know. Did you ever have it where you sort of know something even when you don't really know?"

"Did you ask him if anything was wrong? If he had anything on his mind?"

"I did say it, I asked. But he said no."

"Did he say if there was any special reason he was coming to see you yesterday?"

"No, just that he was going to spend the afternoon with me."

"Look, did he ever mention any of these guys?" He took out his notebook, not trusting his memory. But Sherry stopped him.

"Hold on. Wait a second. Hold on. You're retired, you're not a cop any more. Did Helene hire you?"

"No. Like I told you, I'm just trying to help find him."

Sherry slowly relaxed. "Okay, who?"

"Joe Lippen."

Sherry thought. "Never heard of him."

"Chris Quint."

He slowly shook his head.

"Two brothers. Last name Dalenski. Emil and Mike Dalenski."

"Dalenski," he repeated slowly, frowning. "Yeah, that name. He did mention that name. And I'm sure it was Mike."

"What about him?"

"Oh . . . he said they were playin' pool. And he took this guy for quite a few bucks."

"When was this?"

"When was it? About two-three weeks ago. Right before I had the operation. He thought it was funny because it was years since he shot pool. Like I'd get a kick out of it. Like it would take my mind off my knee. But hell, he could have beat the Pope and it wouldn't have taken my mind off it."

* * *

The sky was heavy with clouds when he left the building, and it was starting to rain. Almost the instant he got in the car, it turned into a downpour.

He wanted to keep going, to find out more about the Dalenski brothers. But he had no idea where they lived, and it was almost six-thirty. He was getting hungry; he hadn't eaten anything since his coffee that morning.

He started the motor and turned on the wipers, waiting to drive because they couldn't clear the downpour fast enough. Water was pounding the hood.

The Dalenskis used to be mean sons of bitches, particularly Emil, the older one and the head of the gang. Actually they were all mean, except for Moogie. He'd been more of a hanger-on, a follower, a not-too-bright kid wanting to be part of something exciting.

And then there was Darla. The stripper with the doll-like oval face and perfect black bangs, Emil's girlfriend. The Lieutenant never quite tied her in with the crimes.

Darla . . . Her last name was Petrone. Darla Petrone.

Sitting there, waiting for the rain to let up, the Lieutenant had no problem remembering her name.

SEVEN

He came home about ten after seven. Ann, standing by the stove, seemed to go limp when she saw him. She closed her eyes for a moment.

"I'm sorry I'm late," he apologized. "I know I should have called."

"That would have been nice."

"I'm sorry, I'm really sorry. But I was busy and I just didn't think of it. Then I got stuck in the rain."

He came over and hugged her. Her arms, reluctantly, slowly came around him. "All right, get washed up and let's have dinner."

She had made one of his favorites, meatloaf with sweet potatoes, but he wasn't as hungry as he'd thought. He was still so geared up he almost had to force himself to eat. Ann didn't ask what he'd done all day: that was her way, to wait. He tried to decide how much to tell her without coming across like a total nut.

"I got an interesting call," he said, "from one of my old informants. About a big robbery."

She looked at him. "Oh?"

"Yeah. I went to see him. And this is what's interesting. His ladyfriend told me he's missing."

"Really?" She set down her fork.

"So I've been looking up people, trying to find out what's happened to him."

She frowned. "What about the police? Do they know about it?"

"Yeah, but they aren't doing anything yet."

"Well, what about the robbery? You told them about it, didn't you?"

"Yes, but that's a little confusing right now. I'm not even sure who was robbed."

"He didn't say?"

How could he tell her the truth, that he just didn't remember? "I'm not sure what he said. It was a little hard to hear him." He felt himself flushing, afraid that he was close to making no sense—and that Ann could tell. "Well, I'll just help her a little more if I can. I'll see."

She kept looking at him with that frown. It seemed to be saying Jack, you're not a cop any more. But she said nothing, and picked up her fork.

"I'll see," he said again.

A little later, after helping with the dishes, he was in the bedroom ready to undress for a shower when he heard his son's voice in the hall. Peter's first words to him were a sharp, "Dad, are you all right?" And then before the Lieutenant could answer: "What happened to the car?"

"What happened to what car? What're you talking about?"

"Your car. The right fender is badly dented."

"What? I'd better look . . ."

"Wait, wait. You didn't know about it?"

"I don't know what you're talking about."

"All right, just take it easy, take it easy." He touched his father's arm. "You have no idea how it happened?"

"No. No."

"Were you parked somewhere? Where were you parked?"

"I—" He suddenly couldn't think of all the places. "I—I was at Westend. The station house."

"What were you doing there?"

"I had to see some people." That's all he'd have to do, tell him what he was doing there! The way Peter was looking at him, interrogating him, was upsetting him.

"And that's the only place you parked?"

"No, I was at a hospital—" He knew he'd forgotten that he'd gone to Moogie's next, but he let it go.

"Which hospital?"

"A rehab place. It's—" But oh no, he was blocked on the name! "A fellow I know is there."

But Peter wouldn't let it stay at that. "Which place?"

"You know the one. You know . . . on Buford Avenue."

Peter kept looking at him. He had his mother's slender build and brown hair, thinning now; he had just turned thirty-five.

"You know, that place on Buford."

"Dad, you had us all worried about you today. Ann called me this morning to tell me not to come over, that you'd left, and then she wanted to know if I'd heard from you, because you still weren't home. You should have let her know where you were going, you should have called."

"I know. I told her I'm sorry."

"You should have let her know."

"Peter, I said I'm sorry!"

"Listen, don't get mad. Please. I'm not your enemy, I'm not trying to hurt you. I want to do what's best for you." He looked at Ann. "Dad, I'd like you to see a doctor."

"What for?"

"Just to go over things. Ann will go with you. Or I'll go with you."

"I'll see."

"What do you mean you'll see?"

"I'll see. Just that. Now stop worrying about me. I'm fine."

Peter took a deep breath. "O-kay."

"Now don't worry about me." He wanted to say: if anything's going to drive me nuts it's this. Instead he said, "And I'll try not to worry about you."

"Yeah."

"Now tell me, how're the kids? How's Joan?"

Afterward, when they were alone, Ann went into the bedroom without speaking to him. It was only then that something formed in his mind that he wanted to shout out:

Baumann Rehabilitation Center!

* * *

Although it was pouring hard again, he couldn't wait to look at his car. He went out into the glistening wet blackness with an umbrella and flashlight. The beam revealed in an instant the large crinkly hollow of the dent; it was just a few inches from the right headlight. He bent over and ran his hand over it, as if he could heal it. But even though he was seething at the bastard who had done it, the thing that was irritating him the most was that Peter was blaming him either way: if he hadn't done it himself, he should have at least noticed it.

He rose slowly, assessing the damage.

And yet—the question was slowly forming—why hadn't he known about it?

He just didn't, that's all. Who the hell always examines the fenders when he gets in and out of a car, especially on the other side?

He started walking back in the rain.

And yet . . . and yet . . . why hadn't he?

* * *

Ann was sleeping quietly while he lay awake, his mind racing. He wondered if Moogie was actually home by now. He wondered, again, how in hell a million- dollar heist wouldn't be all over the news. He found himself reaching once more for the name of the victim, which still seemed beyond the wildest guess. Then his thoughts drifted to Darla. And lingered there.

She'd been no more than nineteen when the gang was rounded up, a "mystery woman" who gave conflicting stories about her background. She had first attracted a lot of attention when she did a gauzy kind of strip at a small club called The

Baron's. He had first seen her during the short time he was in Vice; and though she had the men panting, it was all legal, the pasties and g-string in place; nothing like today. The next time he saw her was after the gang was arrested and he questioned her several times because she was Emil Dalenski's girlfriend. More than that, there'd been indications, though no solid proof, that she knew about the crimes. Then after the five were sentenced, she married the club's owner; when he died, she dropped out of the news. During the past few years she had been showing up in local gossip columns, connected with several medium-sized celebrities.

In all his years on the force he had never touched any of the women who go crazy for cops, and certainly none of the pros. The closest he ever came was with Darla Petrone.

* * *

He slept late for him, till a little after eight. Ann was already up. He must have been dreaming about Moogie: the first thing he thought was whether he had come home after all.

It was too early to call Helene Castle; he wouldn't want to wake her.

He went into the kitchen in his robe and said good morning to Ann.

"Morning," she said. "You feel like cereal? Eggs?"

"No. Just coffee and toast."

"Have you stopped eating?"

"No, I'm just not very hungry today."

He picked up the newspaper and glanced at the headlines, hoping one about a huge heist would leap up at him. After he finished breakfast he went into the bedroom, took out his notebook and called Moogie's number. The line was busy and it was still busy even after he was dressed.

Ann was out on their small balcony, arranging the pillows on the lounge chair, when the Lieutenant came to the doorway and said, "I'm going out for a while. I've got a few more people to see."

She came inside.

"I'll call you if I'm going to be late," he said.

"Jack, let me ask you something. You know I don't butt in, but I've got to ask you. The police aren't in this at all? You're doing this alone?"

"Well, they generally wait a few days before they call something a missing person case."

The answer didn't seem to satisfy her, but she didn't press further. At the door, as he was about to leave, she said, "You take care of yourself."

"Oh, I'm not in any danger. Don't worry about that."

He felt her eyes on him until he closed the door.

* * *

He barely glanced at the dented fender before getting into the car; he was in a hurry to get to Moogie's house. But once he was parked there, he hesitated before going to the door: if Moogie wasn't home he hated to raise even those few seconds of hope. But the door opened slowly, cautiously. Helene's face was solemn.

Without waiting for him to ask, she shook her head.

He said, "Did you try the police again?"

"Yes. They didn't say it but it's like it's still too soon . . . Too soon," she repeated softly.

"I want you to know I tried to call you but the line was busy. I wouldn't have just come."

"Oh . . . my family. But you're not bothering me."

"Look, I asked you this before, but I hope you don't mind my asking again. Dalenski. Two brothers—Mike and Emil. I was talking to someone who said Moogie played pool with one of them a few weeks ago. With Mike. Those names still don't mean anything to you?"

"No."

"I should have asked you this yesterday. But if you hear from Moogie, if you hear anything about him, will you call me?"

"Yes." She said it dully, watching as he carefully printed his phone number on a page torn from his notebook. Her eyes were full of tears. "Mister, Moogie's dead. I just know it. He wouldn't stay away like this. He wouldn't worry me like this. He's dead, I know Moogie's dead."

He tried to offer her a few words of hope, but he was sure she was right.

Now he headed toward the northeast section of the district, only several miles but almost a different world away from his and Ann's apartment; it was the neighborhood where the gang members had lived within four or five blocks of each other, and it had undergone few changes. Although Joe Lippen's and Chris Quint's homes were long gone, the Dalenski brothers' street looked frozen in time. The Lieutenant knew exactly where they had lived; he couldn't forget that day when he and Sarge led Mike down the front steps, hands cuffed behind him and his mother crying.

It was a small apartment, above a laundry. The laundry had been replaced by a small cafe.

He rang the bell and a young woman came to the door holding a baby. No, she never heard of the Dalenskis—there must have been at least eight tenants here in the past twenty-five years—or anyone named Joe Lippen or Chris Quint. The cafe owner said he didn't know any of them, and neither did the only waitress in the place.

He learned nothing at the laundromat on the corner. At the drugstore a few doors away, the pharmacist behind the counter couldn't help him, but an elderly man standing nearby said, "Did you say Dalenski?"

"That's right. Mike. Emil. Brothers."

"Well, Emil's dead if what I heard is right."

"When did you hear this?"

"A couple months ago. I heard some people talking and I remember that name coming up. I remember because they were talking about tough guys and they were saying him and his brother were about as tough as they come, but he died."

"Do you know who these people are that you heard talking?"

"No, I don't. It was in the bar down the street. I was sittin' by myself, but I remember the name because like I say someone said he was so tough."

"Did you ever hear anything about where his brother is living?"

"Nope."

"How about these two guys—Joe Lippen and Chris Quint? Ever hear anything about them?"

The man thought, then shook his head.

"Now which bar did you say this was?"

"Right down the street. Maxie's."

"Thanks." The Lieutenant started to walk away, but stopped. "What about a woman named Darla? Her name was Petrone, but she got married. She used to be a dancer. She'd be in her mid-forties now."

The Lieutenant had mentioned her pretty much as an afterthought, remembering that she might know where some of these guys were.

"No, sorry mister, it don't mean anything."

He tried the bar, but had no luck there. As he was leaving, he noticed a patrol car coming down the street. He kept walking and the car stopped at the curb next to him. An officer with a blond crewcut and thick arms stepped out.

"Pardon me, sir," he said. "Mind if I ask who you are?"

"I do mind, yes. Why?"

"May I see some ID?"

"You may not. No."

"Look, let's try to make this easy for each other, okay?"

"I'm not doing anything. I'm here, I'm standing right here."

"We got a call that someone of your description is harassing people around here."

"What? That's crazy. I'm not harassing anyone. I'm simply trying to locate some people."

"Well, that's the word they used."

"Look." He took out his wallet and handed it to him, open to his FOP card, the Fraternal Order of Police. "I was in charge of this district for twenty-one years."

"Oh?" The officer looked surprised, but only for a moment. "I'm very glad to meet you, Lieutenant, I really am. I'm sorry about this, but a complaint came through and you know, we had to follow up on it."

"I understand. And you were a perfect gentleman."

"Thank you." But he still seemed uneasy. "Now you know I'm going to have to make some kind of report. Can you give me an idea of who you're looking for so I can write something down?"

"Just say I was looking for some people."

The officer's face was slightly pink. "I see. I'll do that."

The Lieutenant stood there as the patrol car pulled away. The report, he knew, would make its way to the second floor of the station house and into the office of Captain Hewitt. And Jack Lehman, or what was left of his reputation, would be forever branded a Grade A crazy.

EIGHT

He watched the patrol car turn the corner down the street, aware for the first time that his heart was beating hard. As he started to walk on he felt a little vertigo. He stopped and closed his eyes and took a deep breath.

To be the enemy! That's what he felt like, the enemy. One of those guys people call cops about, and the cops with their "Hey, buddy. You." How many times had he done that himself! Now he was the "Hey, buddy," the "You."

A big part of him wanted to just get in the car and drive home. But to do what? Go back out there to the pool? To end up going to his grave haunted by this?

He headed toward the sign at the end of the block that said MAXIE'S PLACE. Halfway there he passed a small church, the Church of the First Zion, almost a storefront. It had been a synagogue years ago, and he came there occasionally to say kaddish on the anniversaries of his parents' deaths. It had been a dark little place, surely still was. But it made him think of the synagogue he went to as a kid. He used to hate having to go there three days a week after school instead of being out playing ball. He'd given it up after his bar mitzvah, a poor little business on a weekday in the basement chapel with only his parents there. His father couldn't afford a party, so they hadn't used the auditorium on a Saturday.

He'd come back, somewhat, after his marriage to Trudy, and they gave Peter the bar mitzvah he had never had. He fasted on Yom Kippur and tried to take the day off, though there were times he couldn't, like when those little twins were held hostage by bank robbers. For five years, he had been the head of Shomrim, the Jewish policemen's organization, named for the Hebrew word for watchman. He ate matzo on Passover, bringing it from home when he thought he might be eating at his desk.

He always had the feeling that, after the first looks some of the guys gave each other, they came to respect him for it.

Maxie's Place was long, narrow and windowless. It was after twelve; the long bar was crowded and almost every table was filled. The bartender was middle-aged , his belt low under his hefty belly. The Lieutenant walked to the end of the bar and waited for the man to come to him.

"I wonder if you'd be able to help me out. I'm looking for several people who used to live around here."

"See what I can do," the man said.

"Two of them are brothers. Dalenski? Mike and Emil Dalenski?"

The man shook his head. "Nope. Sorry."

"One's supposed to have died. Emil."

He smiled. "Well, he sure wouldn't live around here any more."

"You got a point. How about these two? Joe Lippen? Chris Quint?"

"No, sorry."

"Just one more. This lady didn't live around here as far as I know, but she used to visit a lot. Darla Petrone. That was her maiden name. Years ago she was a dancer, a stripper."

"No, mister, I'd love to have known her but I don't."

Several people at the bar seemed to be listening to this conversation.

"Well, thanks anyway." There was a phone on the wall near the men's room. A red-faced, heavyset woman at the bar turned on her stool and motioned to him as he was passing her.

"That dancer, that stripper, I'm sure I saw her name. She used to be called just Darla, right?"

"That's right. Where'd you see it?"

"One of the papers, the *Journal* or the *Sun*. I think the *Journal* but I'm not sure. It was in one of those, you know, gossip columns. It said something like how she used to be—you know, an exotic dancer. Called Darla—I remember that, that's what I remember. That name."

"Do you remember anything else it said about her?"

"No, just that."

"When was this?"

"I'm not sure but it was like I'd say maybe a month ago."

He thanked her and walked to the phone, his thoughts shifting between what he'd just heard and the call he was going to make. He wanted to keep on with what he was doing, but he hated upsetting Ann. He wanted her to know that, maybe he should suggest going out to dinner this evening or to a movie.

"Ann, it's me. Just wanted to say hello."

"Jack." She sounded worried. "Where are you?"

"I'm on the street. Something the matter?"

"Jack, Captain Hewitt just called."

"Who?" For an instant the name didn't register.

"Hewitt, Captain Hewitt. From Westend."

"What did he want?" With a sudden heaviness in his chest, he knew.

"I don't know whether he called to talk to you or me, Jack. I really don't. He asked for you and then he started talking to me. He said he was concerned about you, asked how you were, how you were feeling. I told him you were fine, I asked him why he was asking, and he said there was no big reason but he was just a little concerned. Jack, why's he worried about you? What happened?"

"Oh, it's nothing. Nothing at all. A big mixup."

"But what happened? Tell me."

"I told you I'm trying to find someone, and I've been asking questions, and a cop wanted to know what it was all about, and it went upstairs to Hewitt. That's all. But why he made such a damn big fuss . . ."

"Jack, I'll tell you why. He's worried about you."

"But that's silly. Honey, look, everything's all right, everything's fine."

"When're you coming home?"

"Early. Look, don't worry." He lowered his voice. "Honey, I love you. Please don't worry."

"I love you, Jack. That's why I am worried."

"Well, try not to. There's nothing to worry about."

When he hung up, his immediate impulse was to go right over to the station house or put through a fast call to that guy, and tell him he, the Lieutenant, had the goddam right to talk to people without being thought of as a criminal, a crazy. He knew that would be a big mistake; he would probably start yelling and make himself look even loonier. He was about to walk out when he saw someone striding along the bar toward him: a dark-haired husky man in his late forties, tanned and well-dressed in light slacks and a monogrammed sports shirt.

"Okay, what're you up to?" the man demanded.

"Who're you?"

"Never mind who I am! Who're—"

Then he stopped abruptly, and stared in sudden amazement.

"I'll be damned," he said, his eyes widening. "I'll be goddamned. The Lieutenant."

The Lieutenant had recognized him too. Mike Dalenski. Somebody here must have contacted him. And Dalenski must have been nearby.

"Oh my," Dalenski went on with a slight smile. "The fucking Lieutenant."

"Mike," the bartender urged, "how about takin' it outside?"

"The fucking Lieutenant," Dalenski repeated, smiling. "Where's your badge, Lieutenant? No badge? Don't they bury you with a badge?"

"Mike, I just want to ask you a question."

"Ask me a question? Me? You put me away for fifteen years, you bastard. Fifteen years and I never did a thing. Ask me a question?"

"I want to talk to you," the Lieutenant said evenly. "Let's talk outside."

"Yeah, Mike," the bartender repeated. "Take it outside."

"Look." Dalenski ignored the bartender. "Show me a badge and you can go around askin' any goddam question you want. But who the hell are you, old man? And why the hell are you tryin' to hump me? Get off my back! You did enough damage to me, you hear? You hear?"

"I just want to ask you about Moogie."

"Just stay out of my life, you hear me? You ruined it for me once, you took an innocent kid and put him in jail. Now don't fuck with me twice. Whatever you're thinkin', whatever the fuck you're thinkin', I had nothing to do with. So keep my name out of your mouth, okay? Okay?"

He kept glaring at the Lieutenant. Then he whirled and started to walk away, but turned back.

"And keep my brother's name out of your mouth! He's with the saints, which is more than you'll ever be! Don't you ever, don't you ever dare throw filth on his name!"

He strode toward the door.

Now everyone at the bar, the tables, was staring at the Lieutenant. Silently. With hatred.

NINE

HE LEFT THE BAR in time to see Dalenski pull away in his car. His eyes went to the license plate, took in all the numbers and letters, though of course in less than a minute they were jumbled in his mind. His heart was still thumping furiously. He'd wanted to leap for Dalenski's throat, shove him up against a wall, fight to smash in that face even though the years would operate in the bastard's favor. But that would certainly mean the police again, this time probably racing in here with sirens screaming. Long ago he'd learned to control himself when the worst punks, the most vicious murderers, would call him every obscene name they could think of, even when they were in handcuffs. He had always controlled himself . . . except for a few times.

And now he had to just stand there while Dalenski accused him of putting him away for something he never did. Bullshit!

He stood outside the half-frosted window of Maxie's Place. That goddam bartender! He lied, said he never heard of the Dalenskis. But he called out "Mike" at least twice! What the hell else did the guy know, what did the silence of everyone in the bar really mean?

The silence of everyone but the woman who told him about Darla.

She said she'd seen the name about a month ago. That could actually be two months or two weeks. And she wasn't even sure which newspaper it had been in, though she thought it was the *Journal.* That meant he'd have to go to the library and look through the gossip columns in every one of the papers for the past month or so. If it had been in a gossip column. She might even be wrong about that, so he might have to look at the news stories.

But he was remembering something else. He recalled going to a library with Peter and his wife and children for a kids' program called—he couldn't remember what it was called—but anyway, a woman was reading to the kids sitting in a circle, and he and Peter had wandered around and Peter showed him some of the new ways libraries were using computers these days. God, he still didn't know the first thing about a computer . . . even five-year-old Becky, Peter's eldest, even Becky had her own computer, could play games, could probably talk to kids across the world.

He was starting to feel tired and achy, especially his arms, his legs. His muscles had become so tight during that confrontation that everything seemed to be expanding in him now. He was going to continue hitting these streets, every house and store, but he needed to take it easy for a few minutes. He walked to his car a couple of blocks away, locked the doors and turned on the air conditioner. He relaxed against the headrest.

When he was in his sixties, Trudy, may she rest in peace, used to kid him because he often couldn't fall asleep in bed but would nod off reading in a chair or, sometimes for a few minutes in a movie. Ann mentioned it even more, probably because he did it even more.

But he wasn't sleepy now. His mind kept going back to computers. They could do such marvelous things, and it was embarrassing that they were totally out of his world. Peter had offered to show him the basics, but he hadn't seen any need for that, and Ann had said something about where would we put a computer, this place is so small. Now he wondered if he should ask Peter whether he could possibly find Darla's name in the papers. But he didn't think he could really talk to Peter any more; he never knew when his son would get upset with him.

But who else was there? In the old days, when he had reporter friends, he could ask them for just about anything. Now his closest friends there had retired, and anyway he hadn't been in touch with them for years.

He thought about it, and came up with that guy, that writer. He remembered seeing a computer in his apartment. And he was a real nice guy. But what, all of a sudden, was his name? Christ, he was so tired he couldn't think of his name! Was it Newcome? Newcome. No, it wasn't Newcome. Those two damn magazines, he'd taken them out of the car and put them in the apartment—on that shelf in the closet. He even showed Ann where he'd put them. There, he'd said to her, they're right there.

He was anxious to get to them but he didn't want to leave the street yet.

He yawned, covering his mouth, certainly aware he was yawning.

But he wasn't aware of it the second time.

At first he didn't know what jolted him awake, or even that he'd fallen asleep, but through a haze that cleared instantly he saw the barrel of a gun against his window. He jammed himself back against the seat, expecting it to go off, but it didn't, though the barrel stayed there for seconds more. He grabbed the door handle, pushed the door open and tumbled out, falling heavily on his left hand. His whole body seemed to crumple, and it was several moments before he could straighten up and get to his feet. The sidewalk was empty. He began to run, first in one direction and then back. He had to bend over, brace himself against his thighs and draw several deep breaths before he got into the car again and drove to the station house.

There, he walked directly into Captain Hewitt's office. The captain, writing at his desk, looked up with a touch of surprise.

"Jack."

"Captain, some son of a bitch just pulled a gun on me."

He dropped onto the chair next to his desk while the captain watched, frowning. "Where'd this happen?"

When the Lieutenant told him, he said, "Let me see if I got this right. You were sleeping in your car and you woke up and saw this gun."

"Right."

"What woke you?"

"I guess when the gun touched the window. That's the only thing I can think of. Or maybe I just sensed he was out there."

"Did you see the guy's face? Anything about him?"

"No, just his hand."

"A white guy? Black?"

"White, I'm sure white."

"And when you got out of the car, when you fell, you didn't see him running?"

"No. Must have run down an alley or something. I don't know."

"Jack." The captain leaned back in his swivel chair. "Let me ask you this. What were you doing there?"

The Lieutenant took a deep breath. "Remember the call I told you I got? About the heist?"

"I remember. Of course I remember."

"It could be tied up with that. Now I could be wrong, but it's too damn much of a coincidence."

The captain said nothing, was looking at him and waiting for him to go on.

"Remember I couldn't think of the name of the guy who called me? My old informant? Well . . ."

But even as he was saying this, he could feel it slipping away again. Something seemed to clamp shut in his head. He looked down at his lap in a panic, not wanting to meet the captain's eyes . . . Mondo? Monsi? Was it . . . ?

"God," he said, "I'm drawing a blank again."

"Just take it easy, Jack. Just relax. You've just been through a lot."

"I know it like my own—" Then he remembered his notebook. Quickly he took it from his pocket and leafed through the pages.

"Yes. Phil Mondisi," he said, "but everyone called him Moogie. Anyway, I talked to the woman he's been living with. She told me he's been missing ever since he called me."

"What's her name?"

Again a check of his notebook, just to make sure. "Helene Castle. She reported it the next day."

"You know if he ever disappeared before?"

"A couple years ago he did. But that's when he was drinking."

"I see. Well," Hewitt said thoughtfully, "you know how drinkers are. Good one day, good one year, and then . . ."

"She told me he'd never done it again and he never would. Now I'm as skeptical as the next guy, but I believe her. There's something about her I believe."

"Well, even so, you know we don't get all that excited about people going so-called missing for a few days. We'd be up to our ears."

"I know. But there's something else. Now this is before your time." He told him about the Cool Head Gang. "Well, I learned that Moogie was playing pool with Mike Dalenski a few weeks ago, and I've been going around trying to find out where he and the others are living. That's what I've been doing. And just about an hour ago this guy Mike comes into this bar ranting and raving that I was asking questions about him. Said I'd screwed him back then, had sent him up for no reason, which is total crap."

"You think this Mike's the one that pulled the gun?"

"I don't think he'd be dumb enough to try it himself so soon."

"So he might have sent someone?"

"Maybe, though that would be pretty dumb too."

"Then what're you saying?"

"I'm saying I don't know. I'm just saying what happened. Look, it could have been Lippen or Quint too, for all I know.

Someone might have gotten word to them that I was asking about them."

"Or it could have been an attempt to rob you."

"That's true."

The captain kept looking at him. "Jack, let me ask you something. Why do you think the guy didn't shoot you?"

"I guess because I woke up and it scared him, he didn't expect it."

"Come on, he had a gun."

"Maybe he tried but it didn't go off."

"That's possible," he agreed. But he seemed to be saying that it was barely possible.

"All I know is he had a gun."

"Let me ask you this and please don't take offense. How long were you sleeping?"

The Lieutenant looked at him. "I don't know," he said in a firm voice. "But what difference does that make?"

"No difference. I'm just asking."

"I wasn't dreaming this, Hewitt. It was no dream."

"Oh, I know that," the captain answered quickly. "I know."

Oh, sure, the Lieutenant was thinking, staring into his eyes. Oh, sure.

TEN

ANGER KEPT EATING AT him as he headed back to the apartment. A gun, a piece this big pointed right at his head—and for that son of a bitch to even suggest that he might have dreamed it! Dreamed it!

Whoever that bum was he'd either been scared off for some reason or the damn gun jammed. And the odds were it wasn't just somebody trying to rob him; that would be too much of a coincidence. No, if he wanted to stay alive he mustn't buy into a holdup-gone-wrong. He had to act as if someone out there wanted him dead.

Maybe it was the sudden impact of danger; maybe it was the awareness that he would have to be alert every second he stepped out of his building—though God, Ann must never know . . . Or maybe it was just this feeling that he had gone back in time, doing what he loved. But his head felt so clear now. He couldn't remember the last time it felt so clear.

* * *

The first thing he did when he got back to the apartment was call Colin Ryan.

"I'm sorry to bother you, Ryan. This is Jack Lehman."

"No bother at all, Lieutenant. You could never bother me. How are you?"

"Okay. Good. I was just wondering . . . I was wondering if I could ask you for a favor."

"Sure."

"I don't have a computer. I know you have one, and I was wondering if you could find something for me. There was something in the paper about someone I'm interested in and I'm wondering if maybe you could find it."

"I'll try. Which paper's that?"

"Either the *Journal* or the *Sun*, I'm not sure which. It was maybe a month ago. But it could be more, it could be less."

"What do I look for? What's it about?"

"About a woman named Darla. When I knew her, her last name was Petrone. I don't know what it is now. And she used to be a stripper. The story said something about that."

"Do you have any idea if it was a news story or something in one of the columns or a letter to the editor?"

"I was told it was in one of those gossip columns."

"I see," he said slowly. "Look, I can't promise anything but let me see what I can do. Is there anything else?"

The Lieutenant started to say no, then remembered. "I've heard computers can find out where people live. Can you do that?"

"Maybe. It depends."

"I've got these three names. Can I give them to you?"

"Sure."

The Lieutenant took out his notebook and read them off: Joe Lippen, Chris Quint, Michael Dalenski.

"Do you have any idea what city and state they live in?"

"All I know is they used to live here."

"Well, let's see what I can do. I'll get back to you."

"Thanks a lot. I appreciate it. Like I said, I'm sorry to bother you."

"There's nothing to thank me for. I haven't done anything yet. And anyway, I'm being selfish. One of these days I'd like to sit down with you and talk about doing a book on you."

* * *

He woke in the dead of night. Slipping out of bed to go to the bathroom, he saw that the hall nightlight had evidently burned out. He walked slowly through total blackness toward the bedroom door. But he bumped into a piece of furniture which, feeling it with both hands, he recognized to be the bureau. He suddenly wasn't sure if the door was to the right or the left of it. For several moments he thought he was in another room, the bedroom he'd shared for so many years with Trudy: the bureau was in a different place there. He began to feel his way, touched a lamp, then the wall. He began to follow his way along the wall, felt a picture, then another—and finally, the door.

He turned on the light in the bathroom and thought that this was something that could happen to anyone. It had even happened to him, he was sure, before. Still, it was a little unnerving; it made him wonder, just for a few seconds, if the captain could be right.

* * *

Colin Ryan called the next morning. "Well, I have them, Lieutenant."

"Great! Wait, let me get a pencil."

The item about Darla, Ryan said, had appeared in one of the gossip columns. It reported that Darla—her married name was McKenzie—"the former exotic dancer back in the '70s, and one of the town's beauties," had started a public relations agency. And it gave the address. Ryan had been able to get addresses and phone numbers for the three men too. The Lieutenant thanked him effusively.

"Don't mention it," Ryan said. "And remember"—there was a smile in his voice—"I mean it about that book."

But the Lieutenant barely heard him; he was staring at his notebook, wondering what he should do now. The first thing, he decided, was to make sure of the phone numbers. He tried Joe Lippen's first. There was no answer, and he got answering machines at both Chris Quint's and Mike Dalenski's. But a live voice, a young woman's, answered Darla's phone: "Good morning, the Darla M Agency." He quickly hung up, went to the hall closet, opened the bottom drawer of the filing cabinet and took out the gun and the box of shells.

He was kneeling there when he heard Ann's voice behind him. "Jack, what are you doing with that?"

He stood up holding the gun.

"Jack, don't point that."

"Honey, I'm not pointing it. It's nowhere near you."

"What're you doing with it?"

"I'm just going to take it out to the car."

"Why?"

"I just want it there. You know, with everything you read that's going on."

"Jack"—she was staring at him; her voice had become quavery—"I don't like what's happening to you. I'm concerned."

"What do you mean what's happening? Nothing's happening. Except every bum out there has a gun. I just want it in the car."

"But I don't understand. Why didn't you ever want it there before?"

"I don't know. It just hit me."

"Leave it here. Please, Jack. Put it back."

"Honey, I know how to handle a gun. Remember? I was a cop for a million years?"

"Well, you're not one anymore. And you don't need to carry a gun."

"Trust me. I'm asking you. Just trust me."

"Jack, please leave it here."

"Why, for God's sake?"

"Just please put it back. Please. I can't live with you carrying around a gun."

"I'm not carrying it around. It'll be in the car."

"Jack, if you take that with you, I—I'm not going to be here when you come back. I mean it. Put it back."

"Tell me, tell me something. Why don't you mind it here but you do in the car?"

"I do mind it here. I hate it here. But I don't like what's happening to you. I don't like it, Jack, I don't like it."

"What's happening to me?"

"You're just becoming different."

He looked at her. Then, after a long moment, he turned, knelt, and put the gun and bullets back. He pushed the drawer closed. "Okay now?"

"Thank you, Jack," she said. "I mean that."

He looked at her again.

No, thank *you*, he thought. Thank you for my death.

* * *

He looked to either side before leaving the apartment building. And he did the same as he walked quickly to his car. Once inside he relaxed a little, though every so often as he drove he glanced in the rearview mirrors. Tomorrow he'd see, this was crazy, he might take his gun.

Gradually as he approached the downtown area he felt his tension draining away. Not that he was completely at ease, but he felt more the way he always used to feel on a job. Ready. Alert.

He knew this area well, particularly here near police headquarters, which he'd watched being built and where he'd spent so much time. But Darla's address was another matter. He knew it was on the fringe of the city center, on a fashionable side street. He drove slowly through heavy traffic, then soon after it thinned out he saw her street and turned into it. He drove three blocks until he came to her address, one in row of brownstones that had been converted into offices and fashionable shops.

He circled the block twice before finding a spot open almost in front of her building.

But he didn't get out right away; he suddenly wasn't clear about what he hoped to learn from her. It was as though he'd been simply drawn here. He looked at the bronze plaque near the door. It said: DARLA M COMMUNICATIONS. Below it was the name of an insurance agency that was also in the building.

And then he thought: Moogie. Of course. Maybe there was something she could tell him about Moogie.

Her agency, which took up a couple of rooms in her apartment, was right off the vestibule. A secretary who looked like a teenager was sitting at a computer and a woman was standing in front of some files, facing away from him. There were large posters on the walls: old Broadway shows; rock groups; a local nightclub called the Three Dukes . . .

The secretary smiled. "Can I help you?"

"Yes, I'd like to see Miss McKenzie."

The woman at the files turned to looked at him with a pleasant smile. Her hair was auburn now, but she still wore it in bangs and almost shoulder-length. He clearly remembered her peering seductively from behind a curtain before she stepped out on the small stage in that flimsy gauze. And her looking at him alternately soft and hard the several times he had brought her in for questioning. But there was something very different about her now. She was a little heavier—after all, she must be forty-four or -five—but most of all it was the way she was dressed, in a light suit in the cool of this office, and the way she carried herself and smiled.

"Hi. What can I do for you?"

"I was wondering if you could give me a few minutes. I'm Jack Lehman. I used to . . ."

He stopped. Her smile had widened. She said, as if in disbelief, "Lieutenant. My goodness. How good to see you."

"I just want a couple minutes."

"No, no." She led him into a larger room, her office, and closed the door. He sat in the leather chair close to her desk. There were posters on the walls here too.

"Well," she said, still smiling. "It's been how many years, Lieutenant?"

"A long, long time."

"I'd say twenty-four, twenty-five?"

He nodded. "I'd say so. Well, look, I'm not going to take up your time. I just want to ask you something if I can."

"Let me ask you something first. Are you a private cop now?"

"No. No. But I am trying to find someone and I know you knew him. Moogie?"

"Moogie? What's happened to Moogie?"

"He's disappeared."

"Really? Oh, my. But is that anything new? Didn't he used to take off like that?"

"That's what I hear, but his ladyfriend says he hasn't done it since he stopped drinking. And that's been about two years."

"Still," she said.

"Well, she's worried about him. And I have reason to think she's right."

Her expression changed . "But I thought you said you aren't in the business."

"I'm not. It's just that I've gotten involved."

"Well, tell me, how long's he been gone?"

"It's three days now."

"That's a worry," she agreed. "But lots of guys who eventually come home have been away longer than that."

"I know. But this seems different."

"Well, I wish I could help you. Moogie was always a nice guy, although the story used to be he was a rat. If he was he was a nice rat."

She was looking at him as if his face would reveal what he was really after. But the Lieutenant said, without expression, "I heard he was playing pool with Mike Dalenski a few weeks ago. But when I tried to reach Dalenski he came storming after me, said I even sent him to jail for no reason, that he'd had nothing to do with anything."

"He said that?" She smiled slightly. "He did say that?" Then, still smiling, she held out her right hand and turned it, thumb down.

This was another change. This was the same person, Emil Dalenski's girl, who almost never uttered a sentence without saying fuck or shit, and who had denied knowing anything about . . . anything.

"Have you seen Mike lately?" he asked.

"It's been about a couple years. I hear he's still a hothead like his brother, poor soul. But I understand he's doing fine. He owns a limo service, Dalenski Limousines."

"I didn't know that."

"I used to be crazy about Emil," she said reflectively. "Curazy. Of course I was a crazy kid. I was sure we'd get married. But when he went away it seemed it would be forever—fifteen years minimum was like forever—and . . . it just tailed off. He did get married, you know. And just when his wife gets pregnant, he gets leukemia. I went to his funeral. Somehow I had to go. In fact all the fellows were there."

"How long ago did he die?"

"Maybe four years ago. I'd say it's been that."

"Do you see any of them at all?"

"Well, I told you I saw Mike. And I saw Joe a few months ago—you know, Joe Lippen. I just happened to run into him. He does painting, a house painter. But I haven't seen Quinty—Chris—I haven't seen him since the funeral."

"You know what he's doing?"

"I heard he owns a gas station, I don't know where." She leaned back and looked at him with a broad smile. "So, Lieutenant, tell me about yourself. I know you were married. How about kids?"

"Well, my first wife died a few years ago. But I got married again. I've got a son and two grandchildren."

"How nice. I have a son—he's twenty-three. He's out in California. Hollywood. He's had a couple of small parts, but mostly he waits on tables. I give him credit. That's the child I had with Sid Dubin. You remember Sid, of course. The club."

The Lieutenant nodded.

"He died, poor guy. You know it was his idea I become a stripper? I came in there looking for a waitress job, anything, and he must have seen something. He saw that I got lessons, and suddenly Darla is really Darla. Can I tell you something? It sounds corny but I really hated it."

"No one would have guessed."

"I know." She laughed. "I played the innocent little girl who loved to entertain you. Actually I was a little girl from Bozeman, Montana, who had this great urge to get away. It wasn't like there was abuse or anything. I just had to get away. I was sixteen at the time, though that's not the age I gave."

"Good thing you didn't."

"But Sid was good to me, really good. Then it was only five years ago that I met McKenzie—Bill McKenzie, professional rich boy and professional drunk. We're divorced, but I did get to know a few people through him, and I was able to open this business."

"How's it going?"

"Not bad. My big client is the Three Dukes Club, but I've also got a few acts and a couple of stores. We'll see. I have faith . . . You say you're not in the business. But I'm guessing that Moogie's family asked you to find him."

"No, not actually." He wondered how much to tell her. "He called me one morning, said he had something important to tell me. But when I went to see him the next day his ladyfriend said he hadn't been home since the day before. And he's been missing ever since. So I'm wondering what it could be, what he might have been involved in or what he knew."

"And you think"—she frowned—"the boys might be involved?"

"I don't know. I'm just trying to find Moogie."

"I can't believe they're dumb enough to get involved in anything," she said. "Lieutenant, those guys served hard time."

"I know. But a lot of people serve hard time, and come back and serve more."

"Look . . . " she said after a moment.

"Look, what?" he asked.

"I was going to say if I hear anything I'll let you know. In fact, though this scares me a little bit, I probably can get to see the boys again."

"No, I don't want you to do that. Not for this."

"Well, it does scare me, I must admit. They don't scare me, but knowing why I'm doing it . . ."

"I said don't do it . . ."

"I hear you. Okay. But I'm at the club almost every night. And you'd be surprised the things I hear." She smiled. "You're not going to stop me from hearing, are you? You're not going to yell at me like you used to."

"I never yelled." He couldn't help smiling back.

"Oh ho. How about raised your voice then? Well, even when you were raising your voice, you know something? I'm going to tell you something. I fell in love with you. And here's something else. I'm grateful for what you did for me."

He looked at her, puzzled.

"Can I tell you something, Lieutenant? When you took me in and were yelling I was so . . . so fuckin' mad I wanted to kill you. And that was on top of loving you. Anyway, I'm grateful." She was looking at him intently. "And I'll always be grateful. You changed my life. And I owe you."

He kept looking at her, until he realized what she meant. That if he'd pressed harder she would have gone to prison like the others.

ELEVEN

He sat in his car afterward, thinking about Darla. She was right. It wasn't that she'd had a hand in the actual crimes themselves—though he wasn't sure of that either—but that she'd certainly known about them. At the time he'd looked on it as just part of the give-and-take of cop work. Tell us about it, Emil, and your girlfriend's out of it.

Emil had told, at least some of it.

But they already had him and the other guys anyway. The movie theater stub that had led to one of them, their stupid free-talk at a bar, the expensive cars two of them had . . .

He was thinking about her now, not so much the stripper, but the sensual yet fresh-looking girl in tan Bermuda shorts, white blouse and moccasins he'd first questioned in her small apartment. The way her eyes met his, and her smiles and innuendoes, and how at one point he had almost reached out to her, he a man in his forties, a guy in love with his wife, a guy who'd never done that despite all the whores and unhappy housewives and cop-hungry ladies who'd filed through his life. But he hadn't, not then or later, when there were other certain smiles and words, although many nights—this he remembered so vividly—he had carried fantasies of her to his bed with Trudy.

Even now . . .

But he cut that off.

He drove away, suddenly aware that he'd forgotten all about that gun at his window. What kind of senile head did he have if after that he could still just sit in his car like he was sunbathing?

He began looking for a phone, to try to reach Joe Lippen and Chris Quint again. He stopped at the closest parking spot to a phone but once he got to it he realized he had hardly enough coins to make the calls. Not for the first time, he could have kicked himself for not getting a cell phone. Peter had suggested it. But before all this happened, he had felt that he didn't need one; it would be a waste of time and money. Now he was looking around for a place to get change and his eyes set on a storefront with a sign on the window: ANTHONY CARMETTI, M.D. And underneath: FAMILY PRACTICE. The lower half of the long window was covered by a curtain. He went to the door and opened it to see that five or six people were sitting in the waiting room. He closed it slowly and went out again.

He was tempted to go in, but . . .

Doc, am I getting senile? Am I starting to get Alzheimer's?

He didn't know this guy, didn't even know if he could just walk in and see him, like you used to be able to do in the old days. Not knowing the man was what was drawing him there. He didn't want a doctor who would report to someone about him—to his wife, his son, his own doctor—anyone.

But did he even want to know *himself*? He really didn't want to know if he was going flooey. It was better to worry about it than to know, to find out for sure.

He kept looking at the window. Then he opened the door again and this time he walked in. The receptionist was sitting behind an opening in the wall. He walked over to her and asked her in a low voice, "Can I see the doctor?"

"Have you been here before?"

"No." He shook his head.

She frowned and scanned the waiting room. "Well, it'll be a while."

When he nodded, she handed him a clipboard with a paper and pen on it. "Fill out both sides, please."

He sat down and, after struggling to think of a name, printed "Jack Lewis," with a fake address, then checked his wallet to be able to give a zip code, Social Security number and phone number that looked real. He also made up a name and phone number for a person to be called in an emergency.

When the woman at the counter glanced at the paper she frowned. "You don't have Medicare or other insurance?"

"I prefer paying."

"I see. Well, you know it has to be in advance,"

"How much is it?"

"Seventy-five dollars."

He wasn't sure he had that much. But there was seventy-eight dollars in his wallet. He handed her the cash, and watched her count it, before he sat down. No one was looking at him, though he knew they had been.

He waited over an hour before a woman in a lab coat called to him from an inner doorway. At the entrance to the examination room she told him to take off his clothes to the waist; the doctor would be in in a few minutes. It was more like fifteen before he came in, a man in his early sixties with such a warm smile that it was immediately comforting. Almost. The Lieutenant's heart was going fast.

The doctor puzzled over the sheet of paper.

"You're not on Medicare?"

"The card—I either lost it or left it home."

"Be sure to check on that. Do you have any close family?"

"My wife died. I wrote down a friend's name."

"I see. You're not on any medication?"

"I take aspirin. And I take—for urine, for urination."

"Which drug is that?"

The Lieutenant couldn't remember, but when the doctor called off several names, he recognized the one he was taking.

"And you've had just one operation. Gall bladder."

"Yes."

"Good for you. You've got one good medical history." He put the paper aside. "Now tell me what brings you here."

"I—" He didn't know how to say it, didn't want to say it. "I don't remember things as good as I did."

"And that worries you."

"Yeah." He nodded.

"Well, let's see, let's take a look at you."

He gave him a good examination, from his blood pressure—which was surprisingly in the normal range despite his tension—to testing his toes with a needle as he lay on the long table. Then among other things he asked him to walk back and forth, to turn his head from side to side, to stand without moving. Then the doctor sat down with him at his desk.

"Now tell me, young fellow," he said, "do you know my name?"

The Lieutenant looked at him. He hadn't thought of his name from the time he'd walked in that door. "No, just . . . doctor."

"Well, there's no reason for you to remember it. We've just met. Now do you know what day it is?"

"Friday?"

"That's right."

"The month?"

"July?"

"Don't be afraid to say it. That's right. What's your name?"

"Jack . . ." And that was it. What had he changed it to? He felt in a panic. But then, as if the world had opened to him, "Lewis."

And on the questions went, some of which, like who was the president, he was able to answer, and some of which he couldn't. When that was finished, the doctor leaned back in his chair.

"I say you're good for your age. We all lose something of our memory as we get older, you know, and I think you're doing fine."

The Lieutenant almost closed his eyes in relief. He hadn't realized that he'd been holding his breath.

Then he heard the doctor say, "But I'm not a specialist, you know. I feel confident that you're doing all right, but I do think we'll all feel more comfortable—I know I will—if you see a specialist. Now you can go to anyone, of course. But let me give you someone I recommend highly."

As the Lieutenant watched him write on a pad, he felt a sagging within him that was growing heavier by the second. He was back to where he'd started. Maybe even further back.

TWELVE

He was furious at himself for having gone in there. He was furious at that damn doctor for building him up and then crushing him. But most of all, as he drove away, he was worried. He tried to cling to all the good things the doctor had said, but mostly it was that the guy just didn't know; he admitted he didn't know, he said that there was something more to be looked at, that it would take an expert. The Lieutenant was more worried now than when he'd been trying to remember that TV character's name, and trying to remember all those other things, because then it could have all been something he was scaring himself about; it wasn't like a doctor actually saying you'd better see a specialist. It was even a worse kind of fear, though he hated calling it fear, than having that gun at the window because that was something he understood; and it was even worse in its own way than those dangerous situations he'd been in as a cop, because he'd been trained for that; and worse than when he was a kid in the ring, with a guy a head taller and shoulders wider in front of him, because then he could swing back, dance away, go into a crouch and punch in.

Once again he put himself to the test of thinking of all the things he had no problem remembering, like his father's name, his mother's name, and the names of his two sisters who had died. And once again he reminded himself that a lot of things people thought he might have imagined were real, like that damn gun, like his never having been in an accident that caused that goddam dent.

And it was real, oh, was it real, that Moogie had vanished after making that call.

* * *

His apartment had the silence of a cavern. He hadn't wanted to come home, but he'd failed again to reach Joe Lippen and Chris Quint and there was nothing else he could think to do. Ann had left a note on the kitchen table: "At the pool."

He looked in the refrigerator for something to eat and finally made an American cheese sandwich on rye. He took it to the table with a small glass of orange juice poured from a carton. Again he hadn't had lunch, and it was after two o'clock, but he wasn't hungry. He ate because he felt he should.

Afterward he wondered how to spend the rest of the day. He didn't even consider joining Ann and half the building down there, sitting by the pool and suffering through small talk while thinking someone out there was trying to kill him. Even worse in a way, sitting around like that seemed to be one of the steps leading to a nursing home. He would take that gun of his and put it in his mouth if it ever came to that. He wasn't going to be one of those blabbering old goats in a nursing home still dreaming of a Darla and grabbing at every ass or tit in reach.

He walked quickly to the phone, as if propelled, to try Joe Lippen's number again. Reading from his notebook he punched out the numbers—and the voice that answered startled him.

"This is Colin Ryan."

His immediate impulse was to slam down the receiver—he couldn't believe he'd made such a stupid mistake—but he knew Ryan might check and call back. Still, he paused before he said, "This is Jack Lehman."

"Oh, Lieutenant, how are you?"

"I was just wondering . . ." He was trying desperately to think what to say. "You said . . . something, something about getting together."

"Yes, that would be great. Do you know when would be good for you?"

"I . . . I'm not sure yet. I . . . just wanted to say it'll be okay."

"Fine. Great. Look, I can make it any time the next few days. Would it be okay if I call you tomorrow? Or you can call me."

"All right."

"And I can go to your place or you can come here."

"Okay."

"Well, we'll talk tomorrow. It was good talking to you, Lieutenant."

Slowly the Lieutenant hung up the receiver. He looked at his notebook again, saw that Ryan's and Lippen's names were written down near each other—but that was no excuse. None! It was all his goddam head, his head! He kept looking at Lippen's number. Though a big part of him wanted to quit, he tapped it out.

This time Lippen's wife answered.

"No, I'm sorry," she said, "Joe's not home now. He's working."

"When will he be home?"

"I'm sorry, it won't be till late tonight. He's going somewhere after work. Is this very important?"

"Yes, it is. Do you think there's any way I can reach him this afternoon?"

"Tell me, who is this?"

He said, almost starting with "lieutenant": "Jack Lehman. We used to know each other."

"And you say it's important?"

"Yes."

"Can you tell me what it is?"

"It's nothing you have anything to worry about, believe me. I'm trying to locate someone and I think he might be able to help me."

She said nothing for a few moments. Then, "I'll tell you. He might kill me for this, but I'll tell you."

He slowly printed out the address she gave him, then walked quickly to the bathroom where he wet his face, rubbing it hard. As he was heading for the door, he stopped and looked at the hall closet. He thought of Ann and froze, but only briefly. He opened the door, pulled open the bottom and took out the revolver. It was small enough to fit into his right-hand pocket.

* * *

The address was in a suburb that the Lieutenant hadn't visited for several years; he had to ask directions twice before he found the street where there was a small truck parked at the curb and two men on ladders, one on each side of a large Colonial house. The Lieutenant walked over to the older of the two, a man with a gray crewcut and tanned, tattooed arms.

Lippen came halfway down the ladder.

"You want something?"

"I just want to talk to you, Joe."

Lippen frowned. "Who are . . ." Then he almost flinched. "No. I'll be damned."

"I just want to ask you something, Joe, that's all."

"You want to ask me something? Who the hell are you to ask me something! Mister, I'm working." He started back up the ladder.

"Moogie."

Lippen stopped and turned toward him. "What about him? What about Moogie?"

"I want to know if you've seen him lately."

"Seen Moogie?" He gave a half-grin. "No, I ain't seen Moogie. And anyway what's it to you?"

"He's disappeared."

"Well, well, Moogie's disappeared. So what?"

"I was just wondering if you or any of your friends have seen him."

"No," he mimicked, "none of my friends have seen him. They would have called me at any hour of the night—'I seen

Moogie, I seen Moogie.' Sheet. How would I know? Ask them. All I know is I ain't seen him."

"Mike has. Your old buddy. And I thought if he did, maybe you did too."

"I don't care who Mike saw. I didn't see him. I ain't seen him in maybe five years, not that I have to tell you. Look, I gotta work."

He started to go up again, then stopped.

"Look, I don't give two shits what happened to Moogie. King of the stoolies. You think nobody knows that? Hell, he shoulda been shark food long ago. And that's the story from here. Gotta work." He climbed the full height of the ladder and began to dip a brush in the paint can.

The Lieutenant sat for a minute or two in his car. Lippen didn't even glance his way.

What did he expect? The guy to hug the old cop who'd put him away?

He drove off and almost within minutes he realized he had taken a wrong turn somewhere. He tried to guess where he was, made another right but found himself deeper in nowhere. He pulled over and called "Excuse me" to a woman walking by but she just quickened her pace and ignored him. A few moments later he called out to a teenager on a bike, "I'm looking for Route Twenty-One. Could you tell me how to get there?"

"Sorry. We just moved here."

He sat trying to think when all at once a large face was framed in the open window. The Lieutenant's hand flew to his gun-pocket.

"I heard you say," the man said, "that you're looking for Twenty-One."

* * *

He was still feeling rather shaken as he pulled into his parking lot. In all his years as a cop he'd used his gun only once, and that was way back on the motorcycles when this guy was coming at him with a long iron bar; he'd brought him down with a bullet to the stomach that hadn't quite killed him. He'd seen enough ordinary, honest, good people serve time because they'd killed a neighbor they mistook for a burglar, or made any one of a hundred mistakes like that.

The apartment was still quiet. Walking down the hallway, he was horrified to see that he had left open not only the closet door, but the bottom drawer to the filing cabinet. That would be all Ann would have to see! He put the gun back and closed the drawer and the door.

In the kitchen he took out a bottle of water, and reached for a glass. Ann's note was still on the table. Only it wasn't the same note.

"Jack, I can't handle you and a gun. Have to think. Staying at my sister's."

THIRTEEN

HE WAS SO ANGRY with her that for a few minutes he didn't care that she had left. For her to think that he, a cop for all those years, was like a baby with a gun! Like everybody else, she thought he was a senile old fart!

Gradually he began to calm down. She did have this thing about guns, and she had let him keep it closeted away in the apartment. . . It didn't make any sense to him at all—she allowed it to be there but she wouldn't let him carry it. Of course, when she pleaded with him not to take it he had given her reason to think he wouldn't do it. He should have known that Ann, as good and kind as she was, could be like steel when it came to her principles. Just seeing this quiet woman speak at a few Friends' Meetings on issues that were unshakable to her was proof enough of that.

Still, he needed to carry that gun.

He searched their little Rolodex for her sister's number. She and her husband lived about thirty miles away.

"Nora," he said. "Jack."

"Hello, Jack." Then: "Just a second."

"Yes, Jack." Ann's voice was flat.

"Ann, I just don't want you to be angry at me. Please."

"Oh, Jack, I don't know what I am anymore. All I know is I just have to clear my head."

"I understand."

She hesitated and sighed. "Tell me. You all right?"

"I'm okay."

"Jack," her voice brightened a little, "Nora and Art are going to their shore house tomorrow. They want us to come with them for a week. Would you come?"

He closed his eyes in thought. "Ann . . . I've got a few things to do."

"You can't put them off?"

"I really can't. I can't. But you go."

"I'm not going away for a week without you."

"You just go. Maybe, I don't know, maybe I'll drive up for a couple days."

"Oh, Jack. . . Tell me, where's the gun?"

"I have it. I'm not going to lie to you. I'm going to keep it in the car."

He heard another sigh. "Look, I'll decide, I'll see. Anyway I'll be home tomorrow, maybe just to pick up some clothes."

"Well . . . you sleep well."

"Oh, yes," she said tiredly. "Oh yes."

He hung up slowly. It had been so tempting to explain to her why he needed that gun close by, but the story that went with it would make him look even crazier than he did already.

When he went to bed he put the gun on his night table.

* * *

Colin Ryan called him about ten minutes after nine the following morning.

"Lieutenant, I hope I'm not calling you too early."

"No, no. Not at all."

"Listen, one of the names you gave me to look up for you was Joseph Lippen. I don't know if you saw this in today's paper, and I don't even know if it's the same guy, but a Joseph Lippen was murdered last night."

"What?" He was stunned. "I didn't see it."

"It's not on the front page, it's on page three."

"Hold on, will you?"

Part of the paper was still spread out on the kitchen table. He turned quickly to the third page. The story was only about four paragraphs, which could mean it had come in late. But he should have noticed the headline: HOUSE PAINTER SLAIN NEAR BANK. The forty-five-year-old man had been shot around midnight after leaving a friend's house to return home. He had apparently made a withdrawal of $100 at a bank machine and was shot in his car that was parked at the curb. There was a receipt for the money on the floor; his empty wallet was found on the street. No one had seen the killer or killers.

The Lieutenant grabbed up the phone again. "Yes, that's him, that's him." Then he said something he'd heard so many people say after a tragedy: "I just saw him yesterday."

"Really."

"Yeah, he was working at a job. I'll be damned."

" I just wanted to make sure you knew."

"Thanks a lot."

He sat staring blankly at the newspaper page. Robbery. Open and shut. Still . . . murdered. Just a few days after Moogie vanished. One, a guy he'd just talked to, the other a guy he'd just seen. More coincidence? He picked up the paper again.

Just one cop was mentioned, Detective Sergeant Ferron, from Homicide. The Lieutenant remembered him as a brand new detective.

He thought of calling him, just to ask a few questions. Just to try to settle a few things in his mind. But also in his mind was the fear of maybe forgetting names under pressure, stumbling over facts . . .

He called Colin Ryan back.

"Ryan, this is Lehman again. Is there any chance I can see you today?"

"Sure thing, just tell me when."

"I'd appreciate as soon as you can."

"Well, I'd come over to your place now but I'm expecting a couple important calls."

"Look, I would really like to come over, if it's all right."

* * *

As they sat in his living room, Colin Ryan said, "Lieutenant, let me ask you, can I tape this conversation?"

"I don't think there's any reason to. It doesn't have anything to do with my life story."

"Okay. I didn't know."

The Lieutenant looked at Ryan, who was sitting on the sofa with one arm draped across the back and his legs crossed. He was wearing khaki shorts, a polo shirt and sneakers.

"I'm trying," the Lieutenant said, "to think where to begin."

In fact he felt uneasy. Although he trusted Ryan completely, had instinctive faith in him, it took all his courage to tell him, "Some people think I'm going senile."

"Huh?" Ryan frowned and smiled slightly. "I'm no psychiatrist, but I think that if you can say that, then you don't have to worry about it."

"Well, I do forget things. Like names."

"Really? I leave my car someplace and think it's somewhere else. My keys, you don't want to know about my keys . . ."

"Well . . . Anyway . . . I want to fill you in on some things I've told the police about, only I screwed it up right at the beginning. They think I'm completely nuts. But I want to tell you because I trust you and you've helped me and I hope the hell you'll help me some more."

He went on to tell him about Moogie's call and everything he could remember, including his visit to the doctor.

"Ah," Ryan said, "a cautious doctor. Just trying to avoid a lawsuit. You're fine, you know."

The Lieutenant smiled, almost for the first time in days. "I ought to have you call my wife—if I can remember the number." Then he grew serious again. "Do you know this guy from Homicide—Sergeant Ferron?"

"Ferron. Well, sort of. I've spoken to him once or twice. But there are guys in Homicide I really am friendly with. A couple, we're almost like boyfriends."

"Do you think you could ask them some things about Lippen's murder?"

"These two guys I can. I can't swear they'll tell me anything, but Lieutenant, why can't you talk to them yourself?"

"I've told you. They think I'm a nutcase."

"What would you like to find out?"

"If the newspaper story is the whole story. Or if they think he's been involved in anything. I'd just like to know a little about what they're thinking."

"Should I mention Moogie? What he said to you? And that he and Lippen knew each other?"

"Sure. Tell them you and I are friends and I told you all that. Anything you want. And if they want to talk to me, fine. I've tried talking to them."

"Well, let's see what I can do."

The Lieutenant looked at him. "I appreciate this." He reached for Ryan's hand. He had thought he might regret confiding in him, but he didn't, at all. It felt strangely like those days when he knew he'd assigned the right cop to the right job and he could go on to other things.

* * *

The phone rang a few moments after the Lieutenant walked into his apartment. He took the call on the bedroom phone and was surprised to hear Darla's voice.

"Lieutenant, I've been thinking about you. Did you hear about Joe?"

"Yes, I saw it in the paper."

"Yes, I thought you might. It's such a shame. Left two kids—babies."

"I just saw him, by the way."

"You did?"

"Just for a few minutes. He was on a job."

After a silence, she said, "Damn shame. But look, I called you about that, but I'm also calling about a couple other things. You have a few minutes?"

"Sure."

"One, I called Mike this morning. I used Joe's murder as an excuse and he was really friendly, and then I told him—I hope you don't mind—that you came to see me about Moogie. That set him off—'Oh, he had no right to go around asking about me, he isn't a cop anymore!'—but then he calmed down and honest to God he said he was sorry he made an ass of himself. I sort of believe him for whatever that's worth. Anyway . . ."

She paused again.

"Anyway, here's the other thing. I told you I go to this club a lot. It's part of my work—who's there, which celebrities, whose name I can plug. I'm surprised I didn't think of this guy when we were talking yesterday, but he's been in there a few times and last night I think was the third time. He's been hitting on me. Well, he's one of those easy drunks who shoot their mouths off. Talking about all the money he's got, he just bought a Mercedes, and Chuck tells me he really does have a Mercedes and he wasn't worth a nickel a month or two ago."

"Who's Chuck?"

"One of the bartenders."

"Do you know this guy's name?"

"All I know is Larry. He's a blond guy, looks around thirty-five, sort of reminds me of a surfer—you know, hair down to his shoulders. Maybe Chuck or some other people might know more about him. But I've got a favor to ask. If you do talk to anyone there about him, don't let on that we know each other, that anything came from me. That, my friend, could cost me the club as a client."

And maybe, the Lieutenant thought, your life too.

He said, "Honey"—the word just slipped out—"listen to me. I told you this before and I mean it. I don't want to see you taking risks."

"I won't be taking any risks, don't worry. I promise." Then a smile was back in her voice. "Remember I told you I used to sorta kinda love you? Well, don't tell your wife but I still do. I'm still grateful. I always will be."

Then she was gone. His mind travelled back through the years, to that guy they'd pulled from the river, one of their best informants, and another informant with his penis cut off and shoved into his mouth. And of course there was Moogie . . . Moogie.

* * *

He came into the kitchen a few minutes later for a glass of water. And immediately saw the note on the table.

"Jack. I picked up some clothes for the shore. Sorry I missed you. Here is the phone number. Take care of yourself . . . Love, Ann."

God, he'd completely forgotten she was coming home!

FOURTEEN

HE WANTED TO CALL there right away but they were probably still on the road: it was at least a two-and-a-half-hour drive to Ocean City. He decided to wait an hour or two. But in the meantime, what?

Lippen dead. Moogie probably dead. Mike Dalenski a no-talk. The only one he hadn't reached out of that bunch was Quint—Quinty. And then of course there was this guy Larry.

He tried Quint's number again, and almost slammed down the receiver. Always an answering machine! But then he thought of something a friend of his, long dead, used to do; what a lot of people do. He and his wife never answered the phone until they heard who was calling or what it was about. The Lieutenant started to dial again but then stopped suddenly. Leaving his name and phone number would go against years of caution, and if nothing else it would only alert Quinty. But then his right forefinger began to poke at the numbers.

A call came back within a minute. A woman said, "Hello, I'm Mr. Quint's daughter, can I help you?"

"Can I speak to him?"

"He's not here now, he's working, he's at the gas station."

"Would you give me the address?"

"Sure. Who did you say this is?"

"Jack Lehman. We knew each other years ago."

Ten minutes later, his gun in his right pants pocket, he was ready to step out of the lobby door. A few other people were behind him and he stepped aside to let them go first. If there was to be any trouble out there, he didn't want them part of it. Wearing his sunglasses, he waited until they walked across the driveway to the parking lot before he came out too, glancing to each side, his right hand placed casually near his pocket.

Pulling into the gas station, he parked away from the pumps and open bays. As he got out of the car he saw a man standing outside the office, looking toward him. There was no mistaking Quint, even though he was bald now. He was 6'2" or 6'3", with wide shoulders and something of a gut. His eyes didn't shift as the Lieutenant approached him. It was obvious his daughter had called him.

"How are you?" Quint said it with a little smile; a friendly one.

"Good. You?"

"Real well. You look good." He signalled with his head that they should move away from the open door and stand to the side of the building. "So," he said.

"You own this place?"

"Out of hard-earned savings from robbing little kids and stealing dogs."

The Lieutenant remembered Quint as a sort of comedian, even when he was being led away in handcuffs.

"Actually it was my brother's and he died and I got it. So what about you? You look good," he said again.

"Getting by. Getting old."

"Ain't we all."

"I guess your daughter called you."

"My stepdaughter. My wife's daughter. My wife died and I'm living with the daughter and her husband and their kids. They've been very good to me. So," he said, "what's this about? You're not from the lottery, I know that."

"I'm trying to find an old friend of yours. Moogie. He's disappeared."

"Moogie? Really? Well, if you're asking me where he is I don't know. I didn't even know he was gone."

"Had you been seeing him at all?"

"I saw him a few times this year. Mostly he was driving by here and stopped to gas up or just talk."

"When's the last time you saw him?"

"Oh, a few months ago."

The Lieutenant hesitated. But there seemed to be no point in hiding this anymore. "Did he ever say anything to you about a big heist?"

Quint squinted, with a touch of amusement. "Moogie pulled a big heist?"

"I don't think so, but I don't know. You're saying he didn't say anything about a heist?"

"Sorry, no."

"Have you heard about one? I mean a big one. Like about a million bucks big."

"My friend, I was gonna kid you. I was gonna say, like, oh you mean the big one I pulled. But I don't think you're in the mood for kidding. No, I haven't."

"Let me ask you this then. Did Moogie ever say anything about who his friends were?"

"No. Or if he did I don't remember. No. He talked about his lady a lot, what a good broad she is . . . You know something? And this is the truth. I used to hate the son of a bitch. You know, he was a rat. I found that out. Anyways, I get older, I see people, I think of people just trying to get by. And that's Moogie. If you get past the idea that he'd sell you out for a dime, you'll see a pretty nice guy. Well, listen, I got things to do. So unless you have something else . . ."

"Would you let me know if you hear anything?"

Quint smiled. "You mean like a heist? Lieutenant, I ain't no Moogie." His smile broadened. "Who knows?" He started to walk away, but turned back. "I just want to say this. And it's no bullshit. I hated you every second I was in the joint. But I want to tell you something. You did me a favor. If you hadn't said no to me—No, Quinty—I'd be dead by now or serving life."

He touched a finger to his forehead and went back to the office.

* * *

That night he decided to see what he could learn at the Three Dukes Club. He felt good; he'd spoken with Ann and she sounded relaxed, glad to be at the seashore. But on the way, he remembered that he had only a few dollars on him—exactly six. He pulled into the drive of the first bank he came to and parked in the light flooding the ATM machine. No other car was there.

He walked out with a look around, thinking if anyone was after him this could be the place. He inserted his card, but it popped back out. He turned it over and reinserted it, and this time it stayed in, but all at once he wasn't sure which button to press for what account. All these machines were so damn different! He pushed one button, then had to start over with another. The second time, cash came out with his card and a statement.

The Three Dukes was a combination bar, restaurant and dance floor fronting a small, loud rock group. He saw instantly that he was the oldest person there, and the only male wearing a jacket. He took one of the only two seats unoccupied at the bar and ordered a Harps, his favorite though he wasn't much of a beer drinker. He looked in the large mirror at some of the people at the bar. Nobody fit the description Darla had given him. Nobody like that was at any of the tables or on the dance floor.

After about half an hour he ordered another beer. Then he motioned to the bartender. His name-tag said E. Wells. So he wasn't Chuck.

"Do you know a fellow named Larry who comes in here?"

"What's his last name?"

"I don't know. He's sort of a husky guy, about thirty-five, long blond hair."

The bartender thought. "That could fit a lot of people. Sorry. Doesn't ring a bell."

"Will Chuck be on tonight?"

"Chuck? No, Chuck won't be back for a couple weeks. On vacation. This is his first day."

"I see. Thanks."

He sat there for almost an hour longer, nursing his beer, trying to look around without being obvious. Finally there was Darla, in a long tight-fitting dress, standing talking to some people near the dance floor. He hadn't seen her come in; perhaps it had been through the back or a side door. He watched people occasionally approach her; she greeted each one with a smile and almost always, man or woman, with a hug. He watched as she stopped to greet some people at a table. Then a fellow approached her, spoke to her, and led her onto the dance floor. Immediately she became a part of the noisy music scene, smiling up at him, her wrists on his shoulders.

It was crazy, he knew, but he couldn't help this stupid little pang of jealousy.

FIFTEEN

DARLA CALLED HIM THE next morning.

"I just want you to know I wasn't ignoring you," she said. "I saw you sitting at the bar and it was hard not to go over. But I thought of what we'd said about not knowing each other."

"Well, you were right of course."

"When you were leaving I tried to sort of say goodnight with a look but you didn't look my way."

"I'm sorry."

"No, I didn't mean you should have, I didn't mean it that way. I was just saying. Look, I'm also sorry about Chuck. I didn't know he was going on vacation."

"That's okay."

"I felt terrible when I found out. Anyway, there's something else. I forgot to tell you, I don't know how it slipped my mind, but there are a couple women in particular you might want to look up. I saw this Larry having a heavy conversation with them at the bar a few nights ago. Their faces were like this close to each other. I don't know their names but I've seen them there a couple times and I'll be looking out for them."

"Well, you just take care, you be careful."

"Don't you worry, I will. Anyway, I wanted you to know I saw you and I wasn't just being rude. You take care too."

He barely set down the phone when it rang again. He was hoping it was Colin Ryan or Ann, but it was neither of them.

"Morning, Poppy," his five-year-old granddaughter said.

"Hello, sweetheart, good morning. How are you?"

"Good. How are you?"

"Real good. How's your little brother?"

"He's good. But he's a nuisance. As usual. Oh, hold on, hold on, he's such a nuisance. Here he wants to talk to you."

"Poppy."

"Stevie, how are you?"

"Good. I got more dinosaurs today."

"I know you love dinosaurs. I can't wait to see them."

"I can't either. Bye. Here's Daddy."

"Dad, how are you?" Peter said against the background of their voices.

"Good. Fine." He was suddenly uneasy.

"Let me take this in another room." When he came on again Peter said, "So what's new?"

"Nothing. Everything's okay."

"I see. So there's nothing new."

He didn't answer. He sensed what was coming.

"Dad," Peter said. "Ann called me a little while ago. She wanted me to know she's away, that you're alone. Dad, why didn't you go with her?"

"Peter, I've got some things I've got to do."

"You couldn't take off a week?"

"Not right now, no."

There was a pause. "Dad, tell me. Why're you suddenly carrying a gun around? And please don't be mad at her that she told me."

"I'm not mad at her, why should I be mad? And I'm not carrying it around. I'm keeping it in the car."

"But why all of a sudden?"

"Because there's too much crap going on in the streets. And I've got a license, I'm allowed. And a gun couldn't be in safer hands. Remember?—I was a cop, I am a cop."

"Dad," he said it with a sigh, "I'm worried about you, Ann's worried about you, we—"

"Look," he interrupted; and though he never expected to let this out, he did—"you're worried I'm going senile. But let me tell you. I saw a doctor. And he said I'm fine. He tested me, asked me questions, who's the president, who's this, who's that—a lot of questions. And he says I'm fine."

"Who did you see?"

"Some guy, some doctor."

"It wasn't Richman?"

"No, it was someone else. And he's very good."

"Who is he? What's his name?"

Of course he couldn't tell even if he remembered because he had given the doctor a phony name.

"It's just slipped my mind," he said. "I had it and now it just slipped my mind. But I'll think of it, I'll give it to you."

Silence. Then: "Oh Dad."

"I saw a doctor, I'm telling you! Now trust me, believe me. I just can't . . . I just can't think of his name right now."

"Okay. Okay."

He hung up the phone and sat at the kitchen table deeply upset. He loved his son so much and he was sure Peter loved him, but somehow now there seemed to be a real gulf between them.

" " "

His phone rang three more times that morning. The first two calls were from telemarketers; the third, almost at noon, was from Colin Ryan.

"Hello, Lieutenant. I want to tell you I just spoke with someone, Detective Morrison—Ed Morrison? Do you know him?"

The Lieutenant thought. "I've seen his name but I don't know him, no."

"Anyway, I talked with him and he says it's all pretty much what's in the papers. Lippen withdrew a hundred dollars—they know that from the receipt, of course—and he may have been counting it in his car when he was shot. The killer only took cash, left everything else."

"I see. Did you mention anything to him about Moogie?"

"Yes. I told him what you told me. He said that name hasn't come up. But he is interested in hearing more about the heist, he's going to call you about it."

"Good. But they've learned nothing that says Lippen was going sour again?"

"Not so far, anyway. In fact he's been going so clean that even his wife's family started talking to him again. They cut her off when she married him. By the way, her father is Don Reed—you know, he owns that restaurant? Docker's?"

Ryan was saying something about having had dinner there recently, but the Lieutenant hardly heard him. It was as if Moogie was speaking to him again, clear and sharp. Don Reed. That was who Moogie had said was the victim of the heist!

SIXTEEN

DOCKER'S WAS ONE OF the best-known seafood restaurants in the city, a tourist attraction, a place where movie stars, politicians and athletes as well as tourists posed for pictures with a smiling Don Reed. And Reed was well-known for his philanthropy, especially for hospitalized children, and for his Christmas parties for the poor. The last time the Lieutenant had been to Docker's was at least twelve years ago, at somebody's retirement party—Reed had contributed champagne and sat down with the bunch of cops and ex-cops for pictures and laughs.

Him?

The Lieutenant pushed his chair back from the kitchen table, trying to do what he'd always done as a cop when things suddenly seemed too good or too bad: go easy, cool it, look at alternatives. After all, there had to be God knows how many Don Reeds around, not only in the city but in the suburbs—even in the whole damn country.

But his mind kept going back to one point. This Don Reed was Joe Lippen's father-in-law.

But what do you do with it? He thought about going to Captain Hewitt but that guy thought he was cuckoo enough. Maybe he could go to the detective Colin Ryan had talked to, this Morrison who was supposed to call. He could tell him—not that he was sure this was the right Don Reed, that would be crazy, but just . . . tell him.

However, after an hour or so he found himself being pulled in another direction. From what he'd heard, Reed was still the genial host, mingling with his guests. He might be there now. It was a quarter after one.

He had this urge just to see him, to look at him.

It was weird how much you could see into a guy at times, just looking at him.

He stood up quickly and was soon striding, without his usual caution, to his car. It took him about forty-five minutes to drive to the restaurant, which had dark wood and trophy fish on the walls and several bay windows. It had almost emptied out by now. The hostess approached him as he stood looking around for Reed.

"Just one?" She smiled. "Or are you waiting for someone?"

"Just one. Is Reed here?"

"Yes, he's somewhere. Do you want me to get him?"

"No, that's okay."

"Smoking or non?"

"Doesn't matter."

She took him to a table for four; a busboy cleared away three of the settings. The last thing he felt like doing right now was eating.

Reed still hadn't showed up when a waitress came to his table.

"All I'm going to have," he told her, "is a bowl of soup. What do you have today?"

"The soup of the day is crab bisque. But you know we always have snapper."

"I'll have the crab."

The soup came just about the same time Don Reed appeared. He stood talking to the cashier for a few minutes, then made a phone call. He was a medium-sized man about fifty-five, with thinning black hair, dressed in a jacket and tie. The Lieutenant watched him between sips of his soup. Their eyes met once, and Reed smiled. A few minutes later he came over.

"Hi, I'm Don Reed."

"Yes, I know you." The Lieutenant stood up and shook his outstretched hand.

"How's the soup?"

"Good. . .The last time I was here was a long time ago. We had a retirement party for Captain Jenkins. You sat with us, gave us champagne."

Reed thought. "Oh. Jenkins. You a cop?"

"Was. Detective lieutenant at Westend. I was retired myself at the time."

"What's your name?"

"Jack Lehman."

"Jack Lehman," he repeated. "You know, I remember that party. Jenkins and I were good, good friends. Died much too young. But you know, I think I remember you. Jack Lehman. I do."

No you don't, the Lieutenant thought, but he said, "You've got a good memory."

"Just for people," Reed said with a little laugh. "Seriously, I've always felt close to cops. I look on them as special people. I guess it goes back to my granddad. He started this place, you know. And a cop saved his life. Literally."

The Lieutenant nodded.

"If he'd died, it would never have come down to me. But that's a long story. Anyway, I'm interrupting your meal. Happy to meet you, Jack." He held out his hand again. "And let me say this. And believe me. I hope you come back. Soon. And if you have any trouble—reservations, anything, call me. Remember. Anything."

The Lieutenant watched him walk off and stop to say hello at another table.

That guy? Come on. Lost a million?

* * *

There were two messages on his answering machine when he got back. One was from Darla.

"Hello, Lieutenant. Remember the two women I mentioned? I've learned one of them is named Dorothy London. I don't know where she lives but I know where she works. It's called Suzanne's—it's a dress shop on Cower Street near Fourth. Hope it's of some help. Good luck."

The other was from Detective Morrison.

"Hi. Ed Morrison. Homicide. I was speaking with a mutual friend, Colin Ryan, and I'd like to talk to you. When you have a chance, give me a call here. The number is . . ."

But Morrison wasn't in. That was almost a relief. How the hell do you tell him about Reed without coming across like an ass?

SEVENTEEN

HE COULDN'T HOLD OFF any longer. About an hour after leaving another message for Morrison he was driving to Suzanne's dress shop. He was taking a chance that Dorothy London was in; she might be suspicious of just a voice on the phone. The shop was on a street he knew well. It was where Trudy and he had bought their first furniture, and where they had often bought Peter's clothes; but gradually the street had become filled with boutiques and trendy little restaurants, its sidewalks crowded with both the spiked-hair youth and the well-to-do.

A woman was standing at a table folding sweaters as he walked in. She was smartly dressed, with frizzy hair, and looked to be in her late thirties.

"Can I help you?"

"Yes, I'm looking for Dorothy London."

"Well, I'm Dorothy."

"It's good to meet you. My name's Jack Lehman. I'm trying to locate someone; I heard you know him and I thought maybe you'd be good enough to help me."

She frowned. "Who's that?"

"All I know is his first name. Larry."

Her mouth formed a thin little smile.

"A blond guy," he said, "thirty-five or so."

"Oh, I know who you mean," she said with that same smile. "Are you his father?"

"No."

"Well, you should thank God for that." She became serious. "Let me ask. Why're you looking for him?"

"I hope he can help me find somebody."

"Oh, I was sure he owed you money. Or done your daughter wrong, Yes, I know him. Oh, do I know him. I was dumb enough to go out with him. Just once though. He says his name is Larry Samuels. He—"

"Let me write that down."

"I don't think it's going to do you any good."

"Let me write it down. . . Why don't you think it'll do me any good?"

"Because he's a phony. He doesn't live where he said he lived. I know, I checked."

"Where's that?"

"He said he lived—you probably know it, The Hillside, that fancy place." She watched as he wrote it down. "But I told you he's not there, I checked. And he's not even in the phone book."

"Did he mention any of his friends?"

"No." She gave a little laugh. "He was too busy talking about himself."

"Did he talk about having money? I've been told he does."

"He talked yes, oh, yes, but he does have it—or else I can't see straight. He's got a big ring and a watch he says is worth like twenty thousand, and oh, yes he drives this Porsche. I know because I was in it."

"I was told he had a Mercedes."

"No, it's a Porsche. Oh, but he did mention a Mercedes. I remember. But he was kidding. He said he was going to buy it to stand on to wash his Porsche."

"Is there anything else about him you remember?"

"Mister, I'm trying my best to forget him."

"I understand. Well, thank you."

"Good luck." Then, smiling at him as he reached the door, "I can tell you a way to identify him. You look pretty cool to me. He's got a tattoo on his butt."

He smiled back at her. "Thanks."

Driving back, he thought about how many guys he'd busted who had bragged and strutted from a saloon to prison, or who couldn't help throwing their new money at just about everything. But the problem now, of course, was finding this one. He wondered if Colin Ryan could help him again.

One message waited on his answering machine.

"Jack, its me again. Ed Morrison. Sorry we couldn't connect. If you have a chance today, I hope you'll try me again. This time call me on my cell phone."

Hesitantly, still not sure how he was going to handle this, the Lieutenant punched in the number. The answer was almost immediate.

"Ed Morrison."

"Hello, this is Jack Lehman."

"Yes, Jack. Glad we finally caught up with each other. Look, I'm in my car. Would it be okay if I stop over at your place?"

"Sure."

"Great. Hold on just a second, want to get my pen. Yes, give me your address."

"It's . . ." But it was as though his mind had closed on itself. He couldn't think of his street number.

"Jack?"

"Right here. Give me . . . Be right with you."

Desperately he began digging for his wallet in his back pocket, then pushed it back in as he remembered the number.

* * *

Morrison was a compactly-built man in his early fifties, with thick arms protruding from his short sleeves. He settled himself into an easy chair.

"Nice place you have here. Nice building. I thought all retired cops moved to Florida."

"Actually, I did live there for a while, but I didn't like it."

"Really? I'll tell my wife that, she's been talking up Florida.

Anyway let me go over what Ryan told me. A hell of a great guy by the way, a good friend. He's written up a couple of my cases."

Leaning forward, elbows on his thighs and hands locked, he repeated pretty much what the Lieutenant had told Ryan. "Now about Joe Lippen's murder. We don't see any tie-in with this fellow Moogie. I can't say for sure, but I don't think they've even seen each other in years."

"He's still missing, you know."

"I know. I talked to his lady. But just plain missing, you know, isn't my call—at least not yet. But I've passed it along."

"She's already done that."

"I know. Now, one thing I didn't hear from Ryan is who's supposed to have been hit for all this dough?"

"I'm going to give you the name Moogie gave me. . . It's Don Reed."

"Which Don Reed?"

"I don't know. But I heard from Ryan that Lippen's wife is the daughter of Don Reed, from Dockers."

"I know, I—" He stopped and squinted, in a way that was almost a smile, at the Lieutenant. "What you're thinking—you've got to be kidding me now, my friend."

"I'm just saying. Just giving you the name Moogie gave me."

"Let me get this straight. You reported this, didn't you?"

"Of course. I spoke to—" My God, his name, the captain's! "Over at Westend. Where I used to . . ."

Morrison was staring at him, didn't seem about to help him.

"Anyway, at Westend. I told him . . ." Then he remembered. "Hewitt. I spoke to Hewitt there."

"Do you know what he's done about it?"

"No. Look. Let me explain. I wasn't clear on the name then, and I didn't want to give Hewitt a name I wasn't sure of. So I didn't. But when Ryan told me Lippen's wife was related to Reed it was like a bell went off, the name just became clear."

"I see." But the Lieutenant couldn't tell if he really did. Then, after apparently mulling it over, Morrison said, "Let me ask you something else. About the guy who pulled a gun on you. Let me see if I got it right. You were sleeping in the car and you woke up and there was this guy and the gun, and he just took off. And you never saw his face."

"That's right." But he was aware of the doubt in Morrison's voice.

"And you reported it, of course."

"Of course I did." He couldn't help the little show of annoyance.

"So tell me. What do you think? You think someone's after you?"

"I never said that. I don't know."

"I see. Well," Morrison smiled, "if you do I got to hand it to you. You look pretty calm. I don't know if I'd be if someone was after me."

The guy was making a little joke of it. The Lieutenant was tempted to say that he was taking it so seriously he was carrying a gun now; but even though he had a license to carry, he wasn't about to say it. That's all they'd have to know. Fellows, this looney is carrying a piece.

"Well . . ." After a little slap at his thighs Morrison stood up. "Let's see what we can do." He held out his hand and the Lieutenant took it. "You look good, Jack. Really good. Take care of yourself."

It was only after the Lieutenant closed the door that he remembered that he hadn't told him anything about another part to this, the big-mouth big spender. Larry Samuels. But that would only have given him something else to shake his head over.

* * *

The Lieutenant called Colin Ryan soon after the detective left, to ask for his help in locating Larry Samuels.

"All I know is that he told someone he lived in an apartment house here called The Hillside. But apparently he doesn't. In fact he may have even given a phony name."

"Well, let's see what I can come up with."

"Thanks again. By the way, Morrison was just here."

"Good. I hope he was a help."

"He was okay."

But from the way the Lieutenant said it, Ryan was sure it hadn't gone well. And this was confirmed for him only a few minutes later when Morrison phoned him from his car.

"Ed here, buddy. Look, about the Davilion case we've been talking about. I should be able to give it to you in a few weeks."

"Great."

"By the way," he said after a moment, "I just saw our friend, the old man. Look, just between us, how does he strike you?"

This was the real reason for the call. "He seems fine to me."

"Really?" Morrison sounded amazed. "His memory's pretty bad."

"He's a little worried about it, I know. But I think he's great for his age, which isn't all that old."

"I don't know, I really don't. His memory concerns me. Anyway, talk to you again."

Afterward, Ryan's mind kept going back to everything the Lieutenant had confided in him. He was busy, but all he knew was that he wanted to do whatever he could to help. He didn't know if it was because he really believed him or just wanted to believe him. Or just loved and admired a guy who could be reading or napping in the sun but was fighting like hell, even against his old buddies the cops, for his truth.

EIGHTEEN

THE LIEUTENANT HEARD FROM Colin Ryan the next morning.

"I've found a few Lawrence Samuels and a bunch of L. Samuels, but of course you may be right about it being a phony name. Well, I've come up with something else that could be important, but I don't know."

"What's that?"

"I've learned from you guys that a lot of times criminals under pressure will give names that're pretty similar to their own. Am I right?"

"You sure are."

"Well, I called The Hillside and they've got two tenants with names that are somewhat similar to Samuels. One's a Lawrence Sandor, the other's Louis Sammler."

"Hold on, I want to write them down."

"Before you do, Lieutenant, let me ask you something. You're going to look into them, aren't you?"

"Sure, I'm going out there now."

"Well, let me ask you this. You know I've been talking about a book. Well, I'd love to see how you work. What I'm saying is if it's this or something else, I'd like to tag along. I promise I'll stay out of the way."

The Lieutenant thought. "Okay. Fine."

"This one?"

"If you want. But I'd like to leave soon."

"Well, how about if I pick you up? Your place is on the way. And I can leave now."

"All right, if you like." He'd almost always had a driver when he was on active, but other than that he hated being driven around. But for some reason not today.

When he was in the lobby, waiting by the glass doors for Ryan to pull up to the curb, it struck him for the first time that he might be putting the guy in danger. He put on his sunglasses and without hesitation walked out to the sidewalk, off to one side and stood there alone, his hand partly in his right-hand pocket. Cars and vans pulled up occasionally to stop at the entrance. Ryan drew up next to him in a BMW.

Heading off, Ryan said, "I want you to know how much I appreciate this."

The Lieutenant nodded. He suddenly felt awkward about being driven, like he was helpless, like people were right. He wanted to say something, to start a conversation, but he couldn't think of anything.

"This fellow Larry," Ryan said, "is it top secret why you're interested in him?"

"He's just been spending a lot of money he never used to have. I'd like to know whose."

"That's a good reason."

Several minutes passed. He began to feel more comfortable. He liked being with Ryan. It brought back the old days when he'd go out on a case with Sarge or one of the other boys, and there was that something that comes from being with someone you like and trust. Looking over at Ryan, he said, "There's something you don't know I'd like to tell you."

Ryan glanced at him.

"I don't like to give out names unless I'm sure of something. And I'm not sure what this one means. But as you know I trust you. And you're a great help. You know, you're the one told me that Joe Lippen's wife is Don Reed's daughter."

"Right."

"Well, it hit me that that's the name Moogie gave me of the guy who was robbed."

Ryan turned toward him. "That Reed? That guy?"

"I'm not saying that. I don't know. But he did say Don Reed, I know that much."

"You told Morrison about this, I'm sure."

The Lieutenant hesitated to say that he didn't think Morrison cared. "Yes, I did."

* * *

The Hillside loomed ahead of them, a fourteen-story brick building with picture windows and balconies. The tenant list and buzzers were on a wall in a foyer to one side of the glass doors leading into the lobby. The Lieutenant found the two names and marked down the apartment numbers. But he had no intention of buzzing them. He waved to a uniformed man sitting behind the reception desk. After a few minutes the man came out, letting the doors slide closed behind him.

"Can I help you?"

"I'm trying to find someone, and you've got two tenants whose names are a lot like his, and I'm wondering if I got the wrong name to begin with."

"Who's that?"

"Well, one of them's Lawrence Sandor. The fellow I'm looking has long blond hair, is around thirty-five, thirty-six."

"Noo," he said, smiling, "that isn't him. Besides, he's in a wheelchair."

"Oh. What about your Louis Sammler?"

The man thought. "That could be. It's possible."

"Do you know what kind of car he drives?"

"Sure I know what kind of car he drives. But you tell me."

"A Porsche?"

The man smiled. "You got it."

"Would you know if he's in now?"

"No. What I mean is, he left yesterday, he's not in. He stopped at the desk with a suitcase and said he'd be back in a couple days."

* * *

Back in his apartment, the Lieutenant put through a quick call to an ex-cop friend who had a son on the force in Sex Crimes. He asked him to try to find out from his son if one Louis Sammler had any kind of police record.

"I'll be glad to, Jack. But what if he asks why?"

"Just tell him do it. You're his father."

His friend laughed. "Jack, I never thought of that."

The answer that came back later that day was no. This was a blow but there were, after all, such things as first crimes as well as guys with a history of crime they're never linked to. Still, when the phone rang again just a few minutes later, the Lieutenant couldn't resist a dart of hope that his friend was calling back to say there'd been a mistake. But it was Detective Morrison.

"Jack, how are you? How's it going?"

"All right."

"Look, Jack, that Reed—no. No way."

"What makes you say that?"

"We checked, Jack," in a kind of patient, sing-song voice.

"Did you talk to him?"

"No, I didn't, but Lafferty, Major Crimes, did. A good man. Know him?"

No, I don't know him, I don't know him. But he couldn't bring himself to answer.

"So what can I say? You take care of yourself, Jack."

"Yes." He barely heard himself say it. His immediate impulse was to call the guy back, tell him about Louis Sammler. But tell him what? Make an ass of himself again?

NINETEEN

He couldn't believe that they'd done it so fast, had cleared the guy in . . . what? less that twenty-four hours. Why? Because they'd heard about it from a headcase? And added to that, were they so impressed by Reed's reputation, so sure they knew this guy who loved cops and gave to charity and was involved in a million other causes that they hadn't dug at all? But after a few moments he refused to believe that could happen. Except for a toad here and there, a cop was a cop, and they'd obviously had good reason to clear him.

But then which Don Reed was it?

He went to the living room to try to relax enough to think what to do, then began going through his notebook. He picked up the phone to call Moogie's ladyfriend.

An unfamiliar woman's voice answered.

"Can I speak to Helene?"

"This is her mother. Can I help you?"

"I'd like to talk to her if I can. If she's busy or sleeping I can call back. But tell her it's Jack Lehman."

Helene came on, sounding tired. "Yes."

"I'm sorry to trouble you. I just want to ask you one thing. Do you remember if Moogie ever mentioned this name to you? Lou Sammler?"

"No. At least I don't remember it, but I'd say no."

"That's all I wanted to ask."

She didn't say anything. It was as if it was just something else she had to bear.

He said, "Have the police talked to you?"

"Yes. Once. Someone was here." She added in that same tired voice, "He's dead. I know he's dead. I don't care what anyone says, he's dead."

She hung up.

He thought for a moment and then fingered through his notebook and began dialing before he could change his mind.

"Dalenski Limousine Service."

"Is Mr. Dalenski there?"

"No, but he should be back in about a half hour."

She gave him the address and directions to Dalenski's headquarters; he wrote them down, though immediately afterward he had trouble reading his own scribbled handwriting. He wasn't sure if he might do better with that son of a bitch by going there or by just calling him. He recalled Darla saying the guy was a little sorry he blew his top, which meant nothing; he was one of those bums who could always lose it in a second. But that really didn't bother him: he'd been nose to nose with plenty of guys who did everything but drip foam, and sometimes even did that. Mike Dalenski, according to Moogie's friend in the rehab center, was supposed to have played pool with Moogie recently. So which held the best hope of getting him to talk about it, phone or face-to-face?

It wasn't even close.

Dalenski Limousine Service was located on a wide avenue lined with car dealers, the lots strung with pennants and balloons. Dalenski's was little more than a long shack surrounded by stretch limos, vans and a few cars.

Dalenski was sitting behind a counter with another man. When he saw the Lieutenant standing just inside the door he frowned, said something to the man he was with and stood up.

"Weeell," he drawled.

"Mike." The Lieutenant nodded, trying not to show any tension. "I'd like to talk to you for a few minutes. Can I?"

"Sure. Sure."

He led him back to a small office, closed the door and stood leaning back against his desk.

"Before we go any further," he said, "I want to say hey, I'm sorry. I lost my fucking head. Okay?"

"Okay."

"Good. You know, I'm not that kind of guy." He smiled.

"Oh, it wasn't really you."

Dalenski laughed. "Now what can I do for you?"

"It's about Moogie. Do you know he's disappeared?"

"Yeah, I heard."

"I've been told you saw him a few weeks ago, that you played pool with him."

"That's right. So?"

"I just want to know what he was like, was he worried about anything, did anything seem to be bothering him?"

"No, not when I saw him anyway."

"Did you see him often before that?"

"Wait, hold on. I get a turn. Why're you asking? Are you hired by his family?"

"No."

"Then you're not a cop, you're not a private, so I really don't have to answer anything, do I?"

"Mike, you never answered my questions when I was a cop."

Dalenski laughed. "Okay, I like that. What was the question?"

"Did you see him often?

"No. Naah. It was years. We just happened to run into each other and I took him to lunch. One of the things we used to do a lot when we were kids was play pool. So we started talking about it, and there was this place down the corner and we went there. Had a nice time."

"Do you remember him mentioning anyone to you by the name of Lou Sammler?"

"Lou who?"

"Sammler. Lou Sammler."

"No. Never heard the name."

The Lieutenant looked at him. He'd been wondering whether to come out with this name. "What about Reed? Anyone named Reed?"

Dalenski's face didn't change expression. "No. Never heard that either."

"Did he mention anyone else? Any friends?"

"No. No, we just talked about old times."

"Did he say anything about how he was doing?"

"Just that he wasn't working anymore, he hurt his back."

"Let me ask. Do you think he was into anything?"

"Into anything? Oh. Naah. If that's what you're thinking, naah. Moogie was clean. Anyway if he wasn't he never told me."

"Did he ever mention he might know about something?"

"Know about something?" He smiled. "No, he never mentioned he knew about something."

"By the way, did you used to see much of Joe Lippen?"

"Oh, him I did see once in a while. Him I did see," he repeated. "I used to stop over there sometimes for gas. Poor guy. I'll be going to the viewing tomorrow."

Dalenski walked him to the office door. Before he opened it he said, "Lieutenant, remember what I told you about you putting away an innocent kid?"

The Lieutenant looked at him. Dalenski smiled and held out his hand, but only to turn it from side to side.

* * *

He was going to call Ann when he got back, but then, in the mysterious way of couples who seem to anticipate each other, he found a message from her on the answering machine.

He called her immediately.

"Ann, how are you? How're you feeling?"

"I'm fine, Jack. You? Tell me how you feel."

"Good, everything's fine."

"Oh, Jack, it's so beautiful here. The beach. The ocean. Nora and Art, they're marvelous. Jack, won't you be coming down?"

"I don't think so. No, I won't be."

"Oh, Jack. Why?"

"I've just got things to do."

"Oh, Jack . . ." But she didn't finish. She would never plead. But her tone changed. "Well. You do what you want."

"Ann, there's something I have to do."

"Do whatever you want, Jack. Whatever you want. I can't force you."

The apartment seemed emptier, more silent. It was bad enough having to hurt Ann, but what Dalenski said about his not being a cop or even a private eye, wasn't a new idea, but for some reason it was hitting him hard. He found himself starting to forget why he was doing this. An odd thought popped into his head: those little animals, he couldn't remember their name, those little things that once a year ran into the sea. And drowned.

He knew he was acting this way because he wanted to convince everyone, his family, cops, he himself—himself—that what he'd heard he really heard, that he wasn't just some useless old nut. But, too, right up there with it was that a crime had been committed somewhere, a big one involving at least one murder and maybe two that no one even knew about, no one but whoever pulled it and him with his old man's brain.

Just then, repeating in his head what he'd heard seemed to open something for him.

How Moogie had said it. The importance of how he had said it. It made sense all at once.

Moogie didn't say Don Reed, who was such-and-such. Not Don Reed, who . . .

He just said Don Reed. Like Don Reed was someone people knew. Friend of celebrities and politicians. Everyone.

He had to try to find out if Reed had a record. But even if he didn't, that million had to be crud money, from drugs or income tax evasion or a dozen other things. The question was, how could you nail criminals when *their own victim*—their *victim*!—insists there was no crime?

TWENTY

IT WAS NO SURPRISE that a quick check didn't come up with a record. Moments after getting the return call from his friend, the Lieutenant was on the phone again.

"Ryan, me. I'm bothering you again, I'm sorry."

"Lieutenant, I told you before, you can't ever bother me. And in case I forgot I want to thank you for letting me tag along with you."

"You weren't tagging along. You drove."

"I was tagging along. What can I do for you?"

"I'm wondering if you know anyone who knows Don Reed real well. I'm talking about if he has a dirty side."

"Funny, Lieutenant, I've been thinking pretty much along the same line. Actually, I have a couple people in mind, but I need to think about how to work it. Give me a little time. I'll get back to you either way."

He called back about an hour later to say that he had finally reached a friend who knew a little about everything in the city. "We talked about a few things, then I steered it around to Dockers, what he thought of the food, that sort of thing. Anyway, sorry to disappoint, but he had only good things to say about Reed. You know, it's a bigger business than I thought it was. They have some franchises around the country and they're going to be opening more."

"Do you know where Reed lives?"

"He has a farm way out past the suburbs; I can find out where. And he has a condo in town. The only real news is that there was a big hassle a few months ago and he threw his nephew out of the business. I understand it was pretty ugly. The nephew might be someone you could talk to. I know my friend knows him. I don't know how well, but let me talk to him again."

This time Ryan called back within half an hour. "All right. The nephew's named Jeff Rollins. Can you meet him downtown in about an hour? He'll just be leaving work—I hear he got a job with a food wholesaler. He'll meet you in a bar, the Grinning Monkey. It's at Twelfth and Howard."

The Grinning Monkey consisted of a long bar with just a few empty tables. Even though it was after five, only three men were at the bar, two of them talking to each other. The third man, half-turned toward the door, held out his hand as the Lieutenant approached. He looked to be in his mid-thirties, medium height, with curly black hair and blue eyes.

"Jeff Rollins." The handshake was weak.

"Jack Lehman."

"How do you do, Jack Lehman. What'll you have?"

The Lieutenant ordered a Coors. Rollins was drinking Scotch on the rocks. Apparently it wasn't his first. His face was slightly flushed.

"Well," he said, "all I know is that you want to know about my uncle. Excuse me, but you seem to be too old to be a cop. You could be a lawyer or a PI. Or anything," he added with a grin.

"I'm not a lawyer. I'm looking into a private matter."

Rollins held up his hand palm out. "Privacy is my specialty. But I must tell you first that I really love my uncle. Now what do you want to know about the son of a bitch?"

"Is he a son of a bitch?"

"You tell me. It's a mathematical problem. If a guy's a quarter son of a bitch and three quarters okay, what is he? Anyway that's him. I'm his dead sister's only son—her adopted son; maybe that's important, no real bloodline—and I was in the business and I lived at the farm and he threw me out of both places."

He looked down at his drink; both hands were wrapped around the glass. He seemed to forget that the Lieutenant was there.

"Can I ask why?"

"You don't have to ask. I was going to tell you. I'll tell you. I drink a bit. I come in late a bit. But I don't drink all that much and I'm not late all that much, and contrary to what he says I never took a penny from that place that didn't belong to me."

After a pause, the Lieutenant said, "So you're Reed's daughter's cousin. So of course you knew her husband, the fellow who was murdered. Joe Lippen."

"You want to know the truth? I never met him. And that was my uncle again. He didn't want any of us to have anything to do with Dottie or her husband. And I listened. Uncle said something I listened."

"But I hear he reconciled with her."

"That's what I heard. But I'd been kicked out by then."

"When was this?"

"Five months ago. That's when"—he made a dismissive gesture with his hand—"I was out of the farm too."

"Did anyone else live there?"

"Well, he's there, though some nights he stays over in the city. And there was a housekeeper when I was there."

"What's her name?"

"Her name? Mrs. Wells. Megan Wells. Nice lady. A widow. But she's not there anymore either. I don't know why. He let her go before he got rid of me. She'd been with him for years, ever since his wife died. That's at least ten years ago."

"Did anyone else take her place?"

"Not when I was there."

"Did anyone else live there?"

"The past year it was just me and this girlfriend I had then, and my uncle and the farmer—the farmer didn't really live there, he worked there. His name was Fred. I don't know, Fred Something-or-Other."

"Do you happen to know whether your uncle knew someone called Moogie? Real name Phil Mondisi?"

"I don't know. I can't keep track of everyone he knows."

"Or a Lou Sammler? Or Mike Dalenski?"

"They don't mean anything to me."

"Let me ask you—how did your uncle seem before the blowup with you?"

"You mean what was he like? Well, he shows this goddam smiling face to you, to the mayor, reporters, every goddam third-baseman who comes in there, but that's not what he showed me or any of the help who didn't move fast enough."

"Do you know"—carefully—"if anything in particular had been bothering him lately?"

"Just me." He grinned.

"Well, there've been rumors going around that he was taken for a lot of money. I don't know whether it was in the market or he was robbed or what. I'm wondering if you knew anything about that."

"Taken? My uncle?" He laughed. "Never heard it, but whoever took him would have to have mighty fast fingers. Listen, let me just tell you this about my uncle and then I have to leave. It wasn't enough he squeezed my mother out of the business and, oh, gave poor little me a job, but he had a brother who was his partner and you should have seen what he did to his brother's widow. Did I say he's a quarter bad guy? Just increase that . . ."

The Lieutenant paid the bar bill and asked him where he could reach him again.

"Oh, I think I've said it all, mister." That was no surprise. Clearly all he wanted to do was vent his rage on anyone who would listen.

"Well, then what about the housekeeper? You have any idea where I can reach her?"

"Mrs. Wells? Look, I'll do it this way. I'll see if she wants to talk to you, how's that? What's your number?"

"Fine. It's . . ." He restrained a grimace, knowing he would have to go into his wallet. "Ever have anything you know so well slip your mind?"

"Happens to me all the time," Rollins said.

* * *

He didn't have to wait long for her call. It came a few minutes after he walked into the apartment. She didn't give her name. "Mr. Rollins called me and told me what you're after, so I'm calling you."

"Thanks. . ."

"Don't thank me yet," she answered quickly, "because I don't have anything bad to say about Mr. Reed. He's a good-hearted man, was always a good-hearted man, treated me fine, treated everyone fine. And by everyone, that includes Mr. Rollins. I'm not talking behind Mr. Rollins' back, he knows how I feel. He's a fool. And he's a bigger fool to think I would talk against Mr. Reed." She barely paused for breath. "This isn't what you want to hear, I know, people only want to hear the worst of everyone."

"Then why'd you leave?"

"It wasn't his fault, it was that Graywood woman's fault. Said I made up stories about her and him and I—I don't know what else. It was a whole bunch of lies."

"Who's she?"

"You know, from that dance school? She's always in the paper. She put that poison in his mind so what could he do? It was either her or me. I know she was trying to hook him, but the thing is a few weeks later she's out of there anyway. And me, I'm fine, he even saw to it I'm on a nice pension. So I'm saying if you're looking for something bad you're looking at the wrong person."

"Can I ask you . . . ?"

"That's all I wanted to tell you. Just that. He's a good man and Mr. Rollins is a damn fool."

She hung up.

TWENTY-ONE

THE LIEUTENANT APPEARED RELAXED as he sat on his balcony in the morning sun, drinking his coffee and looking down at the spread of lawn and trees. But his mind was on Reed and that former girlfriend of his, Gray Something-or-Other; on the two of them and the nephew and Lou Sammler and—and . . . He went inside, thinking about a second cup of coffee but instead he picked up the phone. He was making the call out of curiosity, not really expecting any answer, but to his surprise a man's voice said, "Hello?"

"Hello?" the voice repeated.

"Yes, is this Lou Sammler?"

"Who's this?"

"My name's Jack Lehman. Is this Mr. Sammler?"

"Yeah. Who're you?"

"I'm looking into something, Mr. Sammler. And I'd like to see you. It has to do with a Mr. Samuels. Larry Samuels."

There was a long pause. "Who are you? What's this about?"

"I'm a former police detective, Mr. Sammler. And as I say, I'm looking into something."

"Tell me what this is about."

"I think it might be best if we talk in person."

"Tell me now."

"I'd like to see you, Mr. Sammler."

Another silence. "Look, okay, but not here. Outside my building. Right outside. The side away from the parking lot."

"Good enough. When?"

* * *

As he made the turn into the driveway, the Lieutenant saw a man with shoulder-length blond hair watching him from the side of the building. As the Lieutenant got out of his car, Lou Sammler took a long pull on a cigarette and tossed it away.

"All right," he said, "who are you?"

"Let's put it this way—who are you? Really."

"What d'you mean who am I? You know who I am. You called me, I didn't call you."

"Come on, let's talk real."

"Look, my wife sent you, didn't she? Didn't she?"

The Lieutenant said nothing, just looked at him.

"I don't understand her," Sammler complained. "We're separated, we're like two inches from a divorce, she's got the kids, I haven't fought her about anything. So I play around a little, once in a while use another name, so what's that to her, so what?"

"Tell me, why couldn't we have had this little meeting upstairs?"

"Guess. You can guess. You weren't always an old guy."

"No, you're right, I wasn't. But tell me, does she know your real name?"

"She knows my real name. Anyway, it's none of your business."

"Well, the way you've been acting, you've made it a lot of people's business."

"Listen, let me just say this, and it's all I'm going to say. If she's worried about my uncle, she doesn't have to be. It's been settled with her lawyer, what more does she want? She gets half. She's not going to be cheated."

"You've lost me."

"Oh, she didn't tell you about the money? What my uncle left me? Like she isn't worried I'm going around spending her share? Come on."

Some fifteen minutes later he was driving back to his apartment. It was weird how you could be at a crime scene with slaughtered bodies and all that blood, and though it could curdle your stomach, it didn't leave you with the same unclean feeling you had talking to some living people.

Suddenly remembering that he needed to buy some groceries, he pulled over to the curb a little past a small food market Ann and he occasionally went to. Mostly they shopped at supermarkets, much as he disliked them. In fact he didn't like shopping altogether, often saying he would never have a new set of underwear if it hadn't been for Trudy and then Ann.

Only a few people were in the place. He picked up a can of coffee and several frozen foods—stuffed peppers, turkey and mashed potatoes, meatloaf and mixed vegetables.

He was walking to the car carrying the bag when he heard a scraping sound behind him. He whirled around as a hand grabbed at his free arm. He saw the blur of a grinning face as he tore free, dropped the bag, and swung wildly. The hand grabbed at his arm again but slipped off, and he saw the man run across the street. Pulling at his gun, he ran after him, between two parked cars, but a group of people were in his way. They scattered at the sight of him but when he got to the other side of the street, the man was gone. He wanted to keep running, but he had to stop, bending over, his breath coming sharp into his lungs. Suddenly there were footsteps behind him. He forced himself to stand up, to run again, but he sank to one knee, his hand straight out holding the gun. It was a beat cop, quickly unhooking his gun from its holster. The Lieutenant opened his fingers and let his weapon drop. The cop pushed it away with his foot.

"Get up."

The Lieutenant rose slowly. The cop patted him down fast. A small crowd stood a short distance away.

"I'm a cop," the Lieutenant heard himself say.

"You're what? You're what?"

"Was a cop." He was still out of breath. "Guy tried to grab me! Grabbed me!"

"Let me see an ID."

The Lieutenant took out his wallet, showed him his FOP card.

"When were you a cop?" The officer was frowning.

"Retired fifteen years ago. A lieutenant-detective."

"I see. I assume"—he said it politely—"you have a license to carry a concealed weapon, don't you?" He had picked up the gun carefully.

"Yes, it's in my car."

"You know of course this is loaded, don't you?"

"Yes. I keep it in the glove compartment."

"Where's your car, sir?"

The Lieutenant led the way, while several people straggled after them. He opened the glove compartment, took out some of the papers, went through them slowly, then took them all out, riffling through them with a kind of desperation.

"I don't know, it's not here. I must have left it in the apartment."

"I see. Now tell me, did you get a look at this guy?"

"Not a good one, no. It happened so fast. I saw a grin but it was weird and I'm thinking it had to be a mask. But it happened so fast."

"A mask?"

"I think so, but I'm not sure." He was aware that he sounded like all the confused victims and witnesses he'd ever questioned.

"Did he have a gun?"

"I didn't see one. But it could have been in his other hand."

"Did he try grabbing your wallet?"

"No, at least he didn't have a chance. Just my arm. But, look, I'm not sure it was robbery at all."

"Why? What then?"

"Someone pulled a gun on me—" he tried to come up with the exact day but couldn't—"a few days ago. I was parked in my car. I don't know if it's the same guy or not."

"They didn't find the person?"

"No."

"Where was this? Who's handling it?"

"It was over at . . ." But he couldn't finish. He inhaled deeply. "The captain there . . ." Again he had to stop.

"Just take it easy, sir. You've been through something."

"It was at Westend."

"I see. You know, sir, I'm going to have to take this gun with me. It'll be at Southeast, where I imagine you can pick it up when you bring in the license."

"But I just told you I have a license. I'm not lying."

"I didn't say you were lying, I never said that. Now can you call someone to drive home with you?"

"No. No, I don't need anyone."

"You sure? This has been quite an ordeal."

"I'm sure, I'm positive!" Immediately he knew he was only making things worse. "I'm really fine. I appreciate your concern, but I'm fine."

"If you say so. And I'm sorry about the gun. I'm sure you have a license. I don't doubt you. But you know how it is. You were a cop yourself once."

* * *

The first place he searched in the apartment was the bureau, where the license had to be. But it wasn't there and it wasn't in the next drawer or the lower ones or in either night table or in the drawers in the living room or the kitchen. He shoved the last drawer shut with his knee. Where the hell was it? No doubt tossed away in one of Ann's mass cleanups. And if there was ever a time he needed a gun!

He knew that the whole thing could actually have been an attempted robbery. But he also knew that he mustn't let it go at that. Believe that and die! But who wanted him dead? Or who, rather, wanted it more—the heisters or their victim?

TWENTY-TWO

HE WENT INTO THE bedroom and sat on the side of the bed. His legs, his arms—everything ached. But what bothered him most was that he'd made a fool of himself in front of still another cop. What a story that guy would tell when he turned in the gun!

His eyes drifted to the answering machine. The light was blinking. He clicked it on.

"Lieutenant, Colin Ryan. I just wondered whether Jeff Rollins called you. Take care."

He was starting to call back when the intercom buzzed.

"Who is it?"

"Is this Mr. Lehman?" a woman asked. "I hope I'm not disturbing you. I'm Detective Alice Valenki from Southeast. I'd like to talk to you. May I come up?"

"Sure." He welcomed it. No detective had showed up at the scene.

He waited for her at his open door. The only female detectives he'd ever known worked at desk jobs, but he didn't have any negative feelings about them being out on the street; he wasn't one of those dinosaurs. In fact he was glad this cop was a woman. It was a refreshing change.

Detective Valenki, a pleasant-looking blonde of about forty, shook his hand and smiled. "I hope you aren't hurt. Did you see a doctor?"

"No, I'm okay, I wasn't hurt."

"I thought maybe you might have been hurt, and of course you know these things can show up later . . . "

"No, I'm all right."

"Can we sit down?"

They settled down in the living room, she with a pad on her lap. "Now I've talked to the officer but if anyone knows the drill, you do. So please just tell me what happened."

He told her that someone he barely saw had grabbed at his arm twice. "All I saw of him—it happened so fast—was a grinning face. At first I thought it was real but afterward I realized it was too weird, it must have been a mask."

"And he just ran off?"

"Well, I swung at him. And I guess this took him by surprise and, yes, he took off. Across the street."

"And you ran after him?"

"Yes, but I lost him by the time I crossed the street."

"And your gun, where was it?"

"I was holding it. I grabbed it as I was running after him."

"And I understand that there were lots of people around there?"

"Not at lot, but there were people."

She set down her pen. "I know I don't have to tell you this. You know that can be dangerous."

He felt the first touch of uneasiness. "My finger wasn't on the trigger.".

"Nevertheless, you know it's dangerous."

"Detective, I was a cop for a lot of years. I think I do know. And I do know how to handle a weapon."

"I'm aware of that. But this is my responsibility."

"And I was attacked, detective. In fact I don't understand why a detective didn't show up and talk to me there."

"I can't explain that either."

"I'm not blaming you. I'm just saying."

"I understand. But I do want to say something else. I know you know this but it's very easy to forget in the heat of the moment. Let's say the person who attacked you was running away in front of you and you shot him. You know you could have gotten in a lot of trouble for that. I know of people who were robbed, whose houses were broken into, and they shot and killed the person while he was running away and they were sent away for murder."

"I know about that too," he said quietly. It was becoming harder to keep the irritation out of his voice.

"I just thought I would remind you. It's so easy to lose your cool."

"Detective"—he couldn't think of her name—"I'm an old hand at keeping my cool."

"I'm sure of that, Jack."

Jack? He was suddenly Jack to her? "I've kept my cool for a lot of years in a lot of tough situations. But now put yourself in my position. You're walking along holding a bag of groceries and someone grabs you. You run after him and, yeah, you do pull your piece because, who knows, he might start coming at you from another way or who knows what the bum'll do to someone on the street. But you still have your head on straight so you keep your finger away from the trigger."

"Oh, yes." But she was already taking another tack. "Now, you never saw a gun. But I see where you thought this was an attempt on your life? Why are you so sure?"

"Did that cop say I was sure of that?" He felt his annoyance turning to anger. "I never said that. I said it was a real possibility. He told you, didn't he, that someone pulled a gun on me a few days ago?"

"Yes, I heard. You were sleeping in your car."

He stared at her. He could tell what she was thinking from the way she said it.

"But I woke up," he said. "I did wake up."

She seemed to be thinking of what else to ask. But he didn't wait.

"When am I going to get my gun back?"

"Oh? Did you find your license?"

"No, I can't find it. But you can check that I have one."

"You have no idea what could have happened to it?"

"No. I can only guess that my wife accidentally threw it out. I know I kept it in a certain drawer."

"What does she say?"

"She's not here, she's in Ocean City."

"You didn't call and ask her?"

"No." He hadn't called because he was afraid it would turn into an argument. "But look, I'll get a copy, it's no big problem."

"Well, it's not up to me, Jack. In fact I don't even know where your gun is."

A goddam lie! And it was so hard just to let it go.

"Jack, let me ask you this. When's your wife coming back?"

Like he needed a keeper! Trying to keep his voice calm: "In a few days."

"Do you have any other family? Children?"

"A son." He said it with a little tremor that only he was aware of. He stood up, wanting to put his face to hers and shout Who are you, a social worker? Instead he said, "A great guy."

"Where's he live?"

"In the city." And the way he said it, she knew that was that.

She seemed a little reluctant to leave, following him slowly as he walked to the door. As he closed it behind her, he wanted to pound his fist against it. Whatever he did only seemed to prove he was a mental case. All he would have to do to finally confirm it was to fly into a rage. If a young person did that it would simply mean he had a quick temper. But in an old person a show of anger would be taken as a sign of dementia.

* * *

The Lieutenant kept looking at the partial name he'd hurriedly jotted down in his notebook after Reed's housekeeper hung up. Gray—and then his mind had shut out the rest. Gray—

what? Greystoke? No, that was Tarzan's real name! Christ, he could remember Tarzan's real name from the time he was a kid, but this name he'd heard just yesterday, only yesterday . . . !

Graywin? Grayman?

He tossed the notebook on the table, then almost against his will tried working out names again. Finally he gave up and returned Colin Ryan's call.

"Yes, Rollins did call me," he told him, "and I met him at a bar."

"Good. I was wondering if he would. Was he any help?"

"I'm not sure. I know he's got quite a hate on for his uncle." He told him about the conversation, and about the call from the former housekeeper. "So, me and my damn head, all I know is Gray Something-or-Other."

"And she teaches dance," Ryan said. "The woman didn't say anything about where? If it's her own school or if she works—"

"Hold on," the Lieutenant said suddenly. "Hold on for a minute. I just thought of something, I want to see something. Or should I call you back?"

"I'll hold on."

The Lieutenant got up and took the Yellow Pages off the shelf. He was amazed that he hadn't thought of this before. He flipped the pages to DANCING—dance companies, dancing instruction.

Then he was back on the phone.

"You still there?"

"I'm here."

"What do they say about overlooking the obvious? It's right here in the damn phone book. Graywood Dance Studio."

* * *

The studio was at the top of a flight of steps amid a row of storefronts. As he opened the frosted glass door, he heard high young voices and saw, through another open door, girls practicing ballet steps. A young woman came out of an office to his left and, after closing the door, asked if she could help him.

"I'd like to see Miss Graywood."

"Is she expecting you?"

"No, she isn't." During the ride there he had thought about how to approach her; he was still feeling his way.

"Just a minute." She tapped lightly on the same door, went in partway, then came out and said with a smile, "All right."

Miss Graywood was sitting at her desk, a tall thin attractive woman who looked to be in her late forties. She asked him with a smile what she could do for him.

"My name's Jack Lehman. I'm a retired detective lieutenant. I'm looking into a missing persons case and it's taking some odd twists and turns."

"I would say so if it brings you here."

"Let me just come out and ask you. Did you ever hear anyone mention a fellow called Moogie? His name's Phil Mondisi but everyone calls him Moogie."

"Moogie. Moogie. How would I know anyone named Moogie? No, I don't know anyone named Moogie." She seemed to be taking it lightly. But then she grew serious. "But how do I come into this? What does this have to do with me?"

"It doesn't have anything to do with you. But I thought you might have been in a position to hear the name."

"Really? Why is that? How did you get my name?"

"Don Reed's housekeeper mentioned you."

"What?" A look of dismay crossed her face. She got up and went quickly to close her office door. "She said I knew this Moogie? She said that?"

"No. She didn't say that. But I told you this thing is taking some twists and turns, and she mentioned that you were a friend of Mr. Reed's."

"Oh, come on! Is she up to her old crap again? She said I had her fired? She's still saying that?"

She went back to her desk but did not sit down for a moment. "That lady—that lady is crazy. Said I was making up stories about her. I never even gave her two seconds' thought! Stories about her! Don wanted to get rid of her long ago and when he did she blamed me. I was to blame. Oh, spare me," she said, raising her eyes apparently toward heaven. "I had no more to do with what happened to her than with what happened to me."

"Can I ask what happened to you?" he asked quietly.

"Nothing. Forget it. Nothing. It has nothing to do with any Moogie."

There was a pause.

"Just," she said, "that he changed. She was out to do over his business, the way he dressed, everything. And I didn't even know what was happening until it was too late and I was out of his life. But he had this PR broad. A stripper yet."

TWENTY-THREE

He stared at her, stunned. "Are you talking about someone named Darla?"

"Oh, you know her? Yes, she has a company called Darla J or Darla N—no, M, Darla M. That woman."

"She has the Dockers account?"

"The last I heard, she didn't. But oh, did she try. He fell for her so hard it's a wonder he didn't go for it. I understand she wanted him to change the whole decor of the place, modernize it—can you imagine? The restaurant's been there almost a hundred years, and people love the look of it, people even know about it all over the world. She even wanted him to change the way he dresses. It would have been a real mess."

"Was this while you were still seeing him?"

"Oh, sure. But of course I was too dumb to get it. I thought it was just business . . . But why am I telling you this?"

"Well, I happen to know the lady. And I'm interested."

She didn't really seem to be listening to his answer; she just wanted to talk about it. "And how did I find out? By accident. I came to the farm unexpectedly and, well . . . *voilà*. And he didn't, you should excuse the expression, give a shit. It was over, done, kaput."

"How long ago was this?"

"I'd say about . . ."

A girl's voice interrupted her from behind the closed door. "Miss Graywood?"

"I'll be there in a minute, dear." Then, to him, "How long ago? I'd say about four months."

"Do you happen to know if they still see each other?"

"I don't know." She rose. "What's more, darling, I really don't care. Honest to God. I really don't care."

"Let me just ask you this. Would you know if he was upset about anything around that time? I've heard that he lost quite a bit of money."

"Mister," she said, "you do ask a lot of questions. If I didn't hate the bastard I wouldn't even answer you. But I have to say that I only wish he did. I don't think he's ever lost a penny in his life, that sweet guy."

She walked with him out of her office and went into the other room with the ballet girls. The inside of his head felt as if it were whirling. Out in the hall he was tempted for a second to take hold of the banister going down, something he rarely did, but he didn't touch it. On the sidewalk the glare of the sun hit hard and he quickly put on his sunglasses.

He walked to his car on a long stretch of sidewalk without a thought of danger, of hands gripping his arms or of grinning masks or guns to his face. He hated to admit it to himself but he felt upset at the thought of Darla with that guy. But even though there was that matter of coincidence again, her being Reed's girlfriend wasn't anything criminal. And, anyway, wasn't she helping him? She'd renewed contact with Mike Dalenski after a couple of years. And after all she was the one, who tipped him off about big-spending Lou Sammler.

But—and it came on though he tried to resist it—just to mislead him?

* * *

He couldn't find a parking spot at first but the second time around the block he saw a car pulling out diagonally across from Darla's building. Here he was close enough to have a good look at whoever went in or out, but far enough away to keep the motor running for the air conditioner without the sound attracting attention over there. He had come here straight from the dance studio. It was almost five o'clock.

He had no idea whether she was in there, perhaps even for the night. But that's how it was with surveillances. He couldn't help thinking of the time years ago—this was like a weird replay—when he and a few of the boys took turns staking out her place on the strong feeling that the now-dead Dalenski brother, Emil, would show up. It had been a tense time for them because that was a gang surely on the road to murder; and when they finally did grab the guy, just as he was walking up the front steps, they had to wrestle with him and then put a gun to his head to stop him, while Darla in the doorway kept screaming, "Don't hurt him, don't hurt him!"

You have, he remembered telling her in his office, bad taste when it comes to guys.

I know, she said, crying.

That was the Darla whom he found attractive. Not the Darla coming through the curtain all gauze and coy smile, taking off one bit at a time down to the pasties and g-string. No—the image kept changing—it was the Darla that time in tan shorts and white blouse, her bare feet in moccasins, and those large eyes in that frame of straight black hair.

He turned off the motor because he was getting low on gas and he had no idea how long he'd be out there. But heat filled the car fast, and he had to turn it on again.

Was it that stakeout at Darla's or another time—there'd been so many—that he had missed the opening day of trout season with Peter? Ever since Peter was six, they'd been going to one of the stocked places with their nightcrawlers and waders, but that time, maybe two years later, he just couldn't make it at the last minute; and the fact that Peter, always such a good kid, never said anything made him feel even more guilty.

He tilted his head slightly, squinting through the sun to see whether the front door was opening. It was. Darla was walking down the steps in shorts, T-shirt and sneakers, a narrow bandana around her auburn hair. Almost the instant she reached the sidewalk she began to run easily, across the street and then away from where he was parked. He watched her disappear beyond some trees at the end of the block.

He waited, with no idea of what he was hoping to learn from this.

After about three quarters of an hour she came back, walking with another woman and carrying some dresses in plastic, apparently having stopped at a dry cleaner. She stood talking for a while with the woman at the foot of the steps. They embraced lightly and Darla walked quickly up the steps and into the building. So ordinary, so nothing.

He made himself wait a specific time longer: forty-five minutes. Then he decided to give it thirty more minutes, exactly. No more, no less. But he didn't have to wait that long. She came down the steps in slacks and low heels, and began to walk down the street. He couldn't see her at first because of all the cars parked at the curb. But then a car pulled out, and he could see her getting into her car. Several moments later, he eased out after her.

He followed a distance behind, just far enough to keep her in sight when other cars came between them. Soon he knew where she was going before she parked. The Three Dukes Club.

She could be in there for hours. He parked and waited about ten minutes before sliding out and locking the doors with the remote.

The club was fairly empty, both the bar and the tables. The band hadn't set up yet. He ordered a Coors at the bar. He wasn't sure what he was hoping to learn from this. It was as though he'd come in for some reason and he'd already forgotten what it was.

But he just wanted to talk to her. To talk to her and look at her.

She appeared a few minutes later from somewhere in back. She stood looking around, then was about to go back again when he slid off the stool and came up to her from behind. "Darla."

She turned, looking surprised. "Why, hello."

"It's okay," he assured her. "New rules."

"Really? Good." She smiled.

"I was in the neighborhood. I thought you might be here and I wanted to tell you about that fellow you mentioned to me."

"You mean Blondie?"

"Yeah. Well, he's just another Romeo."

"Well, I'm sorry I couldn't help you. And lucky me, I didn't date him. Not that I would have—I've seen too many of him. Hims." She smiled. "By the way, I won't be coming here any more. They want too much from me, like every night. I can't put in a full day and come here every night. I've got other accounts and I need time for them."

"Well, good luck."

"Thank you. Thank you very much. In fact," she said, looking at her watch, "I'm going to be cutting out soon. I'm expecting a call from my son's girlfriend. Did I tell you he's in Hollywood? Well, he's on location, believe it or not. Lo-cation. His girlfriend couldn't go with him and she's supposed to be calling me some time tonight."

"Sounds wonderful."

"All my fingers are crossed for him. And my toes. Listen," she lowered her voice, "I got a call from Mike. Didn't say much but, you know, we're still friends. Just thought I'd mention it."

"You just take care."

"You too." She held out her hand and he took it. She smiled at him and then leaned forward and put her cheek against his. "Good night."

"Good night."

He walked out to his car. He sat with the motor off, looking over at the club. He knew he was reliving a part of his life, but oh, how he hoped she was innocent!

* * *

Though he was hungry and thirsty—thirsty most of all—curiosity held him there. After about half an hour she came out and drove off. He followed her along several streets and through several turns, until she pulled up in front of her building. He double-parked a short distance away and watched her walk up her steps. He was just starting to drive away when he saw a figure, a man, walk quickly down the sidewalk and stride up her stairs. The door opened immediately and Darla embraced him before they went inside.

The Lieutenant couldn't see who it was. But he could see that it wasn't Don Reed.

TWENTY-FOUR

He was surprised when he answered the phone late the next morning to hear Darla's voice. "Hello, Lieutenant?" It wasn't just that she was calling, but that there was obvious concern in her voice.

He said, "Is something wrong?"

"No, nothing's wrong. But I'm having a touch of the guilts. I don't know whether I'm doing something terrible."

He said nothing, just waited.

"You know," she went on, "I told you last night that Mike called me. I don't know whether I deliberately didn't mention something or if I just forgot it. And anyway it's probably not important."

"I see. Well, why don't you just let me decide?"

"That's what I made up my mind to do but I still feel guilty. Anyway like I told you, Mike called me. Now I don't know if he thought when I called him that I was coming on to him, which I certainly wasn't. He's married, he's got kids, and I don't need that. But maybe he thought that, because he was like coming on to me. He told me how well his business is doing and then he told me he just bought this big mansion. Now it could all be very legitimate, I wouldn't know, but I promised you . . . Anyway, a part of me really feels awful."

"No, don't. Did he tell you where this mansion is?"

"I asked him. He gave me the address. It didn't mean anything to me and I forgot it. But when I asked him where it was near, he said it was on Malcolm between Ivory and Hill."

"Hold on. I want to mark that down."

"Look," she said, "chances are it's all perfectly legitimate."

"I know. But thanks for the information."

"Well . . . anyway. It was good seeing you last night."

"And you, it was good seeing you."

"So, good luck. And you take care."

"You too."

He sat staring for a long moment at the street names he had written down, but his mind was not really on them. Who was she really? And was she telling the truth or lying to him?

About half an hour later he was heading to the elevator. Although he didn't know if he'd be able to, he wanted to try to see Reed's nephew again. Walking into the lobby he saw a group of elderly residents gathered near the front door. At least two were holding onto walkers. He was approaching the door when one of them, a white-haired widow whom Ann was particularly friendly with, called to him. "Mr. Lehman."

She came over. "We haven't seen your wife around. Where is she?"

"In Ocean City. With her sister."

She smiled. "So those are the parties we hear coming from your apartment."

"Yeah."

"Listen, I don't know if you're interested but you know Ray Macken? He dropped out and we have room for one more person. We're going to take a tour of the Hiller Estate, it's supposed to be very nice, and we're going to have lunch there, and I thought maybe you'd like to join us."

"No, I'm sorry, I can't. Thanks anyway."

The bus was at the curb, its ramp down for wheelchairs. He walked by it quickly. Maybe when he was ninety. No, make it a hundred!

* * *

The lunch crowd was just starting to drift into the Grinning Monkey when the Lieutenant got there. He walked up to an empty stool in front of one of the two bartenders.

"Pardon me. Maybe you can help me. I met a fellow here named Jeff Rollins. Do you know him?"

"Do I know him?" He smiled faintly. "Yeah, I know him."

"I'm trying to reach him again. I'm wondering, is he ever here around now?"

"Sometimes yes, sometimes no. Hard to say."

"Would you happen to have any idea where I can reach him?"

"You don't know?" He said it with a touch of sarcasm.

"No. We'd arranged by phone to meet here."

"You mean today?" He seemed to be enjoying this.

"No, I met him here a couple days ago. And I'd like to talk to him."

"Well, mister, I know where he works, but if he didn't tell you, why should I?"

"Well, would it be possible to call him and put me on the phone?"

"Mister, we're getting busy."

"I know," the Lieutenant said, although it wasn't true. "I appreciate that. But if you could . . ."

The bartender tilted his head slightly. "And you're who?"

"My name's Jack Lehman."

After a minute the bartender walked over to a phone at the end of the bar. The Lieutenant watched him dial, then talk, then dial again and talk some more. He came back.

"He said meet him at the corner of Clayborn and Drew."

"Thanks an awful lot."

The corner was only a few blocks away. The Lieutenant got there first. There was a lot of traffic and pedestrians were crossing at each corner. Finally the Lieutenant saw him approaching half a block away.

"I only got a minute," Rollins announced. "Less."

"Then I'll ask fast. You never mentioned two women your uncle knew. One's a dancer, Graywood."

"Is this what you called me out for? So I never mentioned her, so what?"

"I was wondering if there was any reason you didn't mention her."

"No, there wasn't. She was a nice person as far as I could tell. Very nice. But he always had someone. No surprise she was in, then she was out."

"And there was a woman named Darla, Darla McKenzie. It used to be Darla Petrone."

Rollins frowned. "Who the hell is she?"

"You don't know her? You never heard of her?"

"No, why?"

"I hear she sort of overlapped with Graywood. And I understand she tried to make big changes in his life, in the restaurant, even the way he dressed. For all I know she's still in his life."

"Never heard of her, never heard of it. If it happened it must have happened after I was out of there."

"I see."

"That it?" Even before the Lieutenant nodded, Rollins was starting to walk away. Then he stopped and looked back. "Look, no more of this, okay? No more."

The Lieutenant watched him walk off. He had no idea what he'd hoped to learn; he knew only that he felt a sinking disappointment that he hadn't learned anything more about Darla and Reed. Back sitting in the car with the air conditioner on, he remembered what she'd said about Dalenski buying a "mansion." He wondered how accurate that was. He checked his notebook for the name of the street, and about twenty minutes later was turning into a narrow, cobbled, "no-throughway" road, bordered on both sides by stone walls and palatial homes. There was only one sale sign along the length of it. It stood in front of an arched entrance that led, as far as he could see, past a pond and curved up a tree-lined hill to the pale stone of a huge home. The sign had one word plastered over it: SOLD.

* * *

When he got back he found a message on his answering machine.

"Lieutenant, Colin Ryan. I hate to be the one to keep bringing you bad news. I don't know if you heard but I just learned that a Philip Mondisi was found shot to death. They think it's suicide."

After a moment, he grabbed up the phone, started to dial Ryan's number but couldn't remember it. He took out his notebook and dialed looking at it.

"Ryan, this is Jack. I just got in. Could you tell me anything else?"

"Well, I just saw it in local news on the Internet. They found his car in a woods near the county line. His body was behind the wheel and his gun was right there."

"And they've already ruled out homicide?"

"Well, you know the term they use, 'apparently self-inflicted.' In fact they quoted our friend Detective Morrison."

"Did the story say anything else?"

"No, it was just a little item. But it should be on TV."

The Lieutenant quickly turned on the television set in the living room but the local news wasn't on. He tried an all-news station on the radio in the bedroom. It was almost ten minutes before they got to Moogie. His car had been spotted a couple of days earlier on a rutted lane in the woods, but for some reason no one had reported it or even tried to vandalize it. The body had been found that morning, slumped against the steering wheel, a single bullet in the head. The gun was on the floor. And Morrison was quoted as saying that the wound appeared to be "self-inflicted."

He snapped off the radio, and sat in the silent bedroom. Suicide? But hadn't Moogie's ladyfriend said he'd left the house in good spirits? And hadn't he promised to spend at least part of the day with his friend in the rehab center? What could have compelled him to take the long drive into those woods?

And there was something else.

The Moogie the Lieutenant remembered was one of those guys who could rob you on Saturday and be in church on Sunday. He was never without his St. Christopher's medal. And now, this good Catholic commits suicide?

He tried TV again, hoping something else might have been discovered, but the local news didn't come on until about an hour later, at four o'clock, and after sitting through fires and auto accidents and medical reports and the weather, he still hadn't seen one thing about Moogie's death. Apparently a suicide wasn't big news, at least on this channel. He was trying others when the phone rang.

"Is this Mr. Lehman?"

"Yes." He recognized the voice.

"This is Helene Castle. Moogie's friend."

"Yes, dear. I've heard. I'm so sorry."

"Mr. Lehman, he didn't do it, he didn't kill himself!" She was beginning to cry. "I know he didn't, I know! He wouldn't do that to me, I know it, I know it."

He waited for her to calm down a little. But before he could say anything she said, "And he was so happy the past few days, he really was. And he was really looking forward to seeing his friend. What's more he didn't own a gun. He had a record—you know, he wasn't allowed to buy a gun. How could he shoot himself when he didn't own a gun?"

"And you're sure he didn't get one somewhere?"

"I know I never saw one, I know he never even talked about one."

"Were the police over? I'm sure they were."

"Yes. Yes. And—and I had to go identify him."

Again he waited. "That's tough. That's rough." Then, "Let me ask you. Did you tell the police everything you told me?"

"Yes, why wouldn't I? I'm sure I did."

"And what did they say?"

"Nothing. Nothing. Just—just wrote things down. And then I hear on the news that it's suicide. They didn't listen to a word

I said!"

"Do you know the names of any of the officers?"

"I—I don't know. I forgot. I don't. Mr. Lehman?"

"I'm here."

"You said Moogie was a friend of yours, didn't you? You said he was a friend."

"Yes. Of course."

"And you used to be a detective. So you know those people. You know each other, they respect you. Please talk to them. Try to make them see. Will you, sir? Please?"

"I will. I'll try."

"Please? Please?"

What the hell could he do, he thought as he hung up. How could you prove that Moogie never even owned a gun? That unknown to his lady he hadn't bought one on the street? And if it wasn't his gun, if it was actually planted there by a killer, you sure weren't going to track it down.

He wondered which cop to call to try to find out more. Morrison? Morrison already thought he was senile. Who else? The only other name he could come up with in Homicide was that fellow who he'd read had been the lead detective in Joe Lippen's murder. Sergeant Ferron. The Lieutenant remembered him as a rookie detective.

He picked up the phone.

"Yes," a woman answered, "he's here. Who's this?"

"Tell him it's Jack Lehman. Former Lieutenant Lehman. I used to head up Westend."

"One moment, sir, please." She came back after a couple of minutes. "The sergeant will have to call you back. Meantime he asked if you could tell me a little what it's about."

"Just say I want to ask him something about the fellow who was found shot to death in his car this morning."

"You mean in the woods?"

No, in a balloon! "Yes."

"Would you hold on one more minute?" Then, when she

came back, "The sergeant said for me to tell you the one to talk to is Detective Morrison."

He closed his eyes. "Is he there?"

"Yes, but I see he's quite busy. I'll see he calls you as soon as he's free. Does he have your number?"

"He does, but I'll give it to you."

After waiting about an hour, he called again. The same woman answered.

"I'm sorry, sir," she said when he gave his name, "Detective Morrison just stepped out. I know he'll be back but I don't know when."

He forced himself not to slam down the receiver. A few minutes later he was striding out of the building to his car. He was just going to show up there! But he drove only a few blocks before he pulled over to the curb. This was crazy, this was senile! He sat there, stunned at himself, at his fury.

But he had questions about the suicide! It was such a damn coincidence, like Joe Lippen's murder, and Darla with Don Reed, and Mike Dalenski buying himself a castle.

He started to head back to the apartment, but instead turned off and drove to Darla's street, where again he found a spot with a good view of the door. Darla—Graywood, dumped, hurt, claimed Darla had tried to influence Reed, but Reed's nephew said he had never heard of Darla!

Evening was settling in without anyone entering or leaving the building. He was starting to feel a little sleepy but was sure it would pass—until he woke with a jolt to find that it was dark out and the streetlights were on. He straightened up angrily, remembering how his uncle, his mother's brother, used to fall asleep in his chair, his mouth open. The street was quiet, empty of people.

He decided to give it just a little more time. About fifteen minutes later a car drew up near Darla's place and a man got out, the man he'd seen last night. And this time when Darla opened the door the light from inside illuminated his face. A fan of heat shot through the Lieutenant chest. It was Chris Quint, from the service station. Quinty.

TWENTY-FIVE

I'M GRATEFUL FOR WHAT you did for me, she said.

When you took me in and were yelling at me I was still grateful, she said.

And I'll always be grateful to you, you changed my life, she said.

It was strange: Sometimes he couldn't remember a name he had heard a minute ago, or even something he had just done. But he remembered those words so clearly. Staring at that closed door he was as consumed by the burn of betrayal as he was by the still-growing mystery.

* * *

When he entered his apartment he was surprised to see lights on, couldn't remember leaving them on. Then his wife and son came into the hall from the living room.

"Oh thank goodness," Ann said. "Thank goodness."

"What's the matter?" he demanded.

"What's the matter?" Peter repeated. Then he shook his head at Ann before turning back to his father. "Where've you been? It's almost one in the morning!"

"Out. Just out. Why?"

"Just out." Peter almost breathed out the word. "Look, let's all sit down. . ." Then, leaning forward from his seat on the sofa, "Dad, I got a call from that woman detective. She was marvelous, she—"

"Which detective?" As soon as he said it he remembered.

"You don't remember her?" Peter grimaced slightly. Ann, who was sitting near the Lieutenant, looked pained too.

"I remember, of course I remember."

"Well, you just said you didn't. She was marvelous. She knew you had a son and she was determined to call all the Lehmans if she had to. I was away, I didn't get her message till today, and I called Ann."

"I was coming back tomorrow anyway," Ann said apologetically.

"Anyway she called me," Peter continued. "And she told me you were running after someone with a gun. And in the middle of a crowd."

"Did she tell you why? Did she tell you he attacked me?"

"Grabbed you, yes, she told me that."

"Well, tell me. Seriously. What was I supposed to do?"

"Dad," Peter said, appealing to him. "You were the cop, not me. Tell me, what would you have thought about a civilian with a gun chasing someone through a crowd?"

"But I was a cop. I'm a cop in my blood. I'll always be a cop in my blood. And I didn't have my finger on the trigger. I know better. Give me that."

"But Dad, they took away your gun."

"Sure, because I couldn't find the damn license," he said, turning to Ann.

"Jack," she said patiently, "it's right there. In the bureau. Where it's always been."

"But I looked. And it wasn't there."

"Well, you just didn't look carefully. It's there. It's still there."

He looked at her again, knowing it must be true, but not knowing how it could be—he had looked so carefully.

"So this lady, this detective was concerned enough to track me down and call me," Peter said. "I think she deserves some kind of an award for that. And from what she said I know it's because she honors you, Dad."

The Lieutenant took a deep breath. He didn't know what to say; knew that whatever he did say might be taken the wrong way, would be taken the wrong way.

"Now I want to know this," Peter said. "She said you told her that your life's in danger, that—"

"No, that I think it's in danger." The Lieutenant corrected him.

"All right, you think you're in danger. And you think that someone before this pulled a gun on you while you were sleeping in the car. Why didn't you tell Ann this? Why didn't you tell me?"

"Because I didn't want to worry you. Look, I went through a lot of years not telling my family things that would worry them. And I'm not going to change now. I can't change now."

"Then tell me this. Why do you think it's happening? Why do you think you're in danger?"

The Lieutenant looked at him. He didn't want to go down this road now any more than before; how could he do it without making himself look crazier than they already thought he was?

"I think it may be because someone thinks I'm on to something."

"Dad, please," Peter said impatiently. "Just tell us."

"I did tell Ann some of this. Someone called me, one of my old informants, about a big robbery. And I've been following up on some leads."

"And that's it?" Peter asked, after a pause.

"And there've been a couple deaths that may be connected to it. I don't know."

"Wait, wait! Tell me, where are the police in all this? Did you go to them with it?"

"Of course I did," he said, knowing he could be just about hanging himself here. "But I don't know if they're doing anything."

Peter sighed. "Oh, Dad."

"Peter, I'm not nuts. Believe me, I'm not nuts—"

"Dad, no one's saying you're nuts. But try to listen to me. You're allowed to stop being a cop, Dad. You've given it your best years. But you've got a lot of good years ahead of you when you can just be the great guy you are. These are someone else's headaches. Let them have them. Cool it."

"That's right, Jack," Ann said. "He's absolutely right."

"You've just got to turn off that brilliant brain of yours," Peter said, smiling now. "I mean the cop part of that brilliant mind of yours. Just let it rest, let it relax."

Peter kept looking at him with that same smile. Then, after a glance at his watch, he stood up. "I'd better go home before my wife thinks I ran away."

"You go home," Ann urged. "We'll be doing fine."

Peter came over to his father and hugged him. "I love you, Dad, I hope you know that."

The Lieutenant nodded and hugged him back. "I know you do, and I love you."

After Peter left. Ann said, with a smile, "Hey, what did you eat? I looked through the fridge and there's just about nothing in it."

"I know. I stopped at Walters' and bought a few things but that's where it all happened. I dropped the stuff and I'm sorry, I never picked them up."

"I'm just impressed you shopped."

"Oh, I did a great job."

"I missed you, Jack," she said seriously, "but I just didn't know what to do."

"I missed you too, hon."

She put her arms around him. "Jack, let's try harder. Let's. I love you, Jack. I hope to God you know that . . . Will you try for me, darling?" He knew she meant giving up. "Will you?"

He nodded, hugging her more tightly. He had been so lonely the past few days, and he wasn't lonely any more. It felt so good not being lonely. But he couldn't shake off thoughts of that mystery out there, and Darla's shadow over it.

TWENTY-SIX

HE HAD A GOOD NIGHT'S sleep, the first in days. It was good too to sit down to breakfast with Ann, and later, though they were in different rooms, to feel her presence in the apartment. Still later, when she had to go food shopping, he joined her as usual; he still didn't enjoy it, but he liked being with her. And after lunch, when she suggested going out to the pool, he got into his swim trunks without being urged a second time.

In the pool area there was just a scattering of people on the lounge chairs. A few mothers were watching their children in the kiddies' pool, and in the shallow end several elderly women and men were determinedly walk-exercising from one side to the other. He dived in from the far end, and began his slow, fluid crawl along one of the lanes reserved for laps. He did eighty, though he could have gone on and on, and then climbed out on the shallow end, and toweled off.

Several acquaintances had pulled chairs close to theirs, and two of the men reached up to shake his hand. They were a few years younger than he.

"Looked good there, Jack," one said. "Looked real good."

"How many did you do?" the other asked.

"I'm not sure."

"Really? Looked like at least forty."

"I don't know. Maybe." He did know, of course, but he hated to sound like he was bragging.

He sat down and put on his sunglasses but not Ann's sun lotion. They were talking about the condo fees; had he heard the rumor that they'd be going up? He said no, he hadn't, and the conversation turned from the maneuverings of the condo board to Caribbean cruises and then to the stock market. He lay back, closed his eyes and, though he'd been fighting them all day, let the thoughts come.

You were a detective, Helene Castle had said. *You know those people, they respect you, please talk to them, try to make them see.*

He squinted his eyes shut tighter, as if to shut out her words.

Yeah, they respected him, oh yeah! Not even to answer when he called or call him back.

A loony!

He opened his eyes and watched the walkers in the water, new ones now, some of them vigorously swinging their arms from side to side as they walked. One of the men was telling his friend, "Did I tell you I got glaucoma? Thank God for eyedrops."

"No. A lot of people I know have it. But tell me, do they let you drive?"

"God, yes. That's all that would have to happen."

"I think that's really the end when you can't drive."

"Jack," one of the women said, "you were sleeping. A short snooze, but a good one?"

The Lieutenant nodded.

"I can sleep everywhere but in bed," somebody said, with a laugh. "Movies. Living room chairs. But not the bed."

The Lieutenant smiled but he couldn't wait to get out of there. These were nice people, it was nice being out here, but it was taking willpower just to sit here until he could walk together with most of the group to the elevators.

Ann showered first while he waited in his robe in the bedroom. Then, thinking of it for the first time today, he walked over to the bureau and opened the drawer, staring into it, stunned. For there it was, the license, under a large box of old cufflinks, buttons and collar studs that he had picked up in his search and must have set aside to search below it maybe half a dozen times.

He found himself clutching his head, trying to hold it together.

Please talk to them. Try to make them see. Will you, sir? Please?

TWENTY-SEVEN

ANN TOOK THE PHONE call when it came right after breakfast. "Yes," she said, and turned to him. "It's for you."

"Hello?" Aware that Ann was watching him from the sink.

"Mr. Lehman?" It was Helene Castle. "It's me again, Mr. Lehman. I hope you don't mind. But I just had to ask if you'd talked to anyone yet."

"No, I haven't been able to reach anyone."

"Oh. Okay. But you will keep trying?"

"Yes."

"I just know he didn't kill himself, Mr. Lehman. I must sound like a broken record but I know he didn't."

"I understand." He hated himself for sounding so stiff, but Ann was there. "I'll talk to you soon. All right?"

"Yes, thank you. And God bless you. I want you to know I'm sorry. Please excuse me."

"That's all right."

"Thank you. And again I'm sorry."

Ann didn't ask who it was. She had turned on the water and was running the garbage disposal. When she was finished he said, "You know that fellow I told you was missing? That was the woman he lived with."

"Oh, yes."

"They found him shot to death—he's one of the two dead people in this thing I mentioned. The cops think it was suicide but she doesn't believe it."

"Oh?"

"She wants me to talk to the boys," he said hesitantly. "She thinks I can help convince them to look into it again."

"And are you going to?"

He looked at her. "Ann, I got to. I promised."

She put the breakfast dishes in the dishwasher, sponged off the sink, then wiped off the table. He knew she was fighting not to say anything.

"It won't take much effort," he said. "Maybe just a phone call, I don't know. But I promised."

She still said nothing. When she opened the closet to take out a mop he went into the bedroom to dress. His eyes went to the bureau drawer. He had tried convincing himself that it could have happened to anyone, that it *did* happen to the young, old, middle-aged, whatever, when they're in such a hurry they can't see things right in front of their eyes—their glasses, car keys, you name it. But it didn't help. He should have seen it, it was right *there*.

He wanted to take the license and go retrieve his gun. But he could see them calling Peter or telling each other, *the old guy's got his gun back!* And he was afraid of losing Ann for good.

* * *

He must be an idiot! Such a simple, simple thing! It struck him late that morning as he was trying to watch television, switching channels and now turning it off altogether. Here he'd been trying to figure out how to get Morrison at Homicide to at least listen to him, not look at him as a senile old fool for at least a few minutes. Now he realized that it wasn't only Homicide he should be talking to. If anyone had any lingering interest in the case, it would be the district where the body was found. The Northeast.

Ann was in the bedroom, running the vacuum sweeper. He went to the phone in the kitchen, reached a detective at Northeast, introduced himself and asked if he could speak to whoever investigated the death of Philip Mondisi.

"What's your name again, sir?" It was as though it had all come through too fast.

"Jack Lehman."

"Hold on."

It was almost five minutes before someone came on. And it was with a burst of enthusiasm. "Is that you, Lieutenant?"

"That's right. Who's this?"

"George Brewer. I hope the name still means something to you. It's been a long time."

It took a few seconds before the name separated itself from all the others in his life. And then: of course! He'd tapped George, a patrolman, to go undercover making drug buys when he was only a year or so on the force.

"George, it's good talking to you. How are you?"

"Good, Lieutenant, good. Great talking to you. How've you been?"

"Good. Can't complain too much."

"Great! So tell me, what can I do for you? I hear it's about that fellow Mondisi."

"Yes, I'd like to talk to you about it."

"Well, let me ask you. I was just on my way out, I've got something to do that can't wait. Can this hold for a few hours? Or, say, how about meeting me for lunch in about an hour? My treat. I'd really like to see you, Lieutenant, it's been a long time."

"Yes, I'd like that." He could speak freely; Ann was still in the bedroom.

It was easy to spot George in the luncheonette, even before he stood up from his table and held out his arms. He looked the same at forty-nine as he had at twenty-two, though his hair was graying and he'd put on some weight. He grinned, embracing the Lieutenant hard and gestured him into the chair across from him.

"It's so good to see you, Lieutenant. You look good, you really do."

"You do too, George."

"Naah, got fat. And by the way"—he smiled—"I don't play the sax any more."

The Lieutenant smiled back at him. That was one of the things he'd screened for in making that undercover assignment. His man had to be able to get enough decent sounds out of the instrument to win the confidence of a music store owner they suspected of fencing a lot more than instruments. And it had worked.

"You gave me a big break," George said. "I'll always remember that."

"You really did it on your own."

"Well, whatever. The point is, you showed confidence in me. I might still be walking a beat."

"I doubt that."

After they ordered—the Lieutenant wanted just a sandwich and coffee, George the roast beef platter—George said, "So tell me. What about this Mondisi?"

"First of all, the guy used to be a stoolie of mine."

"Really? That's a surprise."

"I hadn't seen or heard from him in years. But then just the morning he disappeared he called me and said he'd heard about a million-dollar heist. "

"You're kidding! When was this? Where?"

"Well, from what he said it already happened, I don't know when. All I know is I haven't heard anything about it and no one else I've talked to has heard of it either. He did give me a name but I'll get back to that.

"Now I imagine," he went on, "you heard that Mondisi's nickname was Moogie. Well, he was part of a gang we put away a little before your time. They've all been released. One of them died a natural death, but two others, Moogie and a guy named Joe Lippen, died within about a week of each other. Lippen was murdered in what the boys say was a holdup, and now we have Moogie."

"What about the rest of them?"

The Lieutenant told him about Chris Quint and Mike Dalenski, and that Darla had been Emil Dalenski's girlfriend. "And I do know," he added, "that Chris Quint and Darla see each other. At least they've seen each other once that I know about. Are you clear on this so far?"

"I've got it."

"Now, what I didn't tell you before. When he called me, Moogie gave me the name of at least one of the people who was robbed. It—"

Suddenly the name was gone. As George looked at him, frowning, his mind seemed to be burying it even deeper.

"I—I'm sorry, I'm drawing a blank."

"That's okay, Lieutenant, it happens, just take it easy."

"Drawing a goddam blank."

"It'll come to you."

"My God." He held right hand fingers to his forehead, as if to squeeze out the name. "You'll have to exc—I'm sorry."

"That's okay. Just relax."

"Anyway," the Lieutenant said, drawing a breath, "this Joe Lippen who was supposed to have been killed in a holdup, his wife's sister . . ."

And there was that name again.

"Give me a minute, just give me a minute."

"Lieutenant, you don't even have to do it today."

"Let me think, let me think." And then, something opened in his head: "Don Reed! That's the name Moogie mentioned! You know, the guy who owns the restaurant. And Joe Lippen's wife is Don Reed's daughter."

George frowned and glanced at the next table. "You saying you think he was robbed of a million bucks?"

"I'm only telling you what Moogie told me."

"But he didn't say which Don Reed."

"No, but it was like I should know."

"Like you should know?"

"I mean he didn't say which one he was. It was like it didn't need an explanation."

Their orders came, but George seemed not to notice.

"Have you told this to any other cop?"

"Yes." But he didn't even try to think of a name. "But they said he was never robbed."

"They said that," George said.

"I don't know what they based it on. Maybe they talked to him, I don't know. But I do know what Moogie told me."

"But you say he never did say which Reed."

"But I'm telling you why I believe it's him."

George kept looking at him. "I see. Now about Moogie's death. What about it?"

"The lady he lived with swears he would never commit suicide."

"Oh, Lieutenant, how many times have we heard that?"

"I know, I know. But they were talking about getting married, he was going to cheer up a friend that day—"

"I know, Lieutenant. I know all that. I talked to her. I talked to the lady."

George was looking at him with a little smile. It was probably meant to be kind and reassuring. But it was as though this man who once admired him, and perhaps still did, was trying to help him gently down some steps.

* * *

Ann hadn't asked him where he was going and when he came back she didn't ask him where he'd been. She seemed determined to separate herself from that part of him, to spare herself pain and to keep peace. She did ask whether he'd had lunch, and he said yes, he'd met a guy who once did some work for him.

"Well, I'll be going out to the pool," she said. "What about you?"

"I don't know, I'll see."

"I spoke to Lori." One of her two married daughters. "She had to keep Debbie home from day camp, she has a sore throat."

"Does she have a fever?"

"A little, not much."

He wondered how well he was hiding it from her, that his thoughts were mostly elsewhere. He had felt a little strange mentioning Darla to George, as though he were accusing her of something when he really wasn't sure. After all, there were so many conflicting things about Darla: the Graywood woman accusing her of trying to manipulate Reed, his nephew saying he'd never heard of Darla; and Darla herself letting him know about Mike Dalenski buying a mansion. Why would she do that? Because she knew he'd probably find out anyway?

The intercom buzzed. Ann said, "There's a package downstairs for you. I'll get it."

She came back from the lobby holding a manila envelope. "A process server handed it to me," she told him, frowning.

He looked at it with a slight sinking feeling: it was from a law firm and he couldn't think of any way this could be good. When he opened it the first words leaped up at him:

"This office has been retained to represent Donald T. Reed with regard to the attached complaint. Please note that you have been sued in a court of law and that damages are being sought against you for allegedly slandering Mr. Reed . . ."

TWENTY-EIGHT

HE WISHED HE DIDN'T have to stand there trying to read it with a worried Ann looking on. He didn't even try to read all of it, skimmed through enough to find out the unbelievable: that Reed's suit was based on his talking to Jeffrey Rollins.

Rollins! The guy who claimed to hate his uncle so much! Nothing in the complaint about the housekeeper or ex-girlfriend Graywood.

And it said he had just twenty days to file an answer—or he could "lose money or property or other rights important to you."

"Jack, what is it?" Ann was saying. "Can I see it?"

He handed it to her. "I'm being sued."

"By who?" She didn't even begin to look at the papers.

"Some guy named Reed. Don Reed."

"Jack, tell me. Who is he?"

"You know, the robbery. The guy who told me about it, Moogie, told me who was hit. He said Don Reed. And I had reason to tie it up with this Don Reed."

"Jack, you're not being clear at all. He mentioned the name Don Reed. But which Don Reed are you talking about?"

"He owns that restaurant. Dockers."

She stared at him. "Dockers? And you know it was him?"

"Ann, everything points to it."

"But can you prove it?"

"No, not yet."

"Not yet? And you've been going around accusing him?"

"No. But I did ask some questions."

"But you slandered him. It says here that you slandered him."

"I told you, I asked some questions."

"Oh my God! Oh, Jack, you've really done it."

"Give me the papers, please." He reached for them.

"Oh," she said, "now what're you going to do?"

"Get a lawyer."

"And what're you going to do, sue him back?"

"Ann. I've got to defend myself."

"How will you do that? You say you can't prove—You say you can't prove it."

"I don't know. I have to talk to a lawyer."

Her cheeks were pink. "Jack, I'm worried. This could, it could ruin us."

"It won't ruin us, it'll work out."

"Really?" She nodded quickly, in a way that said she knew better. And it was, he knew, her way of fighting against anger. "I hope so."

He went for the phone book. As he turned the pages he was doing his own fighting, against losing control, something he couldn't recall ever happening even on his most dangerous job as a cop. But then there had always been something that was still in his power, something he could do. Now it seemed that if he let go he would be free-floating.

He used to know a million lawyers, most of them assistant D.A.s or defense attorneys. The last time he hired a lawyer was about eight years ago when his car was hit from behind at a red light. He wasn't sure of the lawyer's name anymore, just that it began with Ne or Me. He went through the Yellow Pages twice before stopping at Lebower, Stuart. That was definitely it.

He got through to him on his first try.

"Mr. Lebower, I hope you remember me. Jack Lehman. You represented me—"

"Sure I remember you. The detective, the lieutenant. What can I do for you?"

"I want to know if you handle this sort of thing. I'm being sued for libeling someone. I—"

"You mean you published something about someone?"

"No, I'm sorry. They say I talked about someone, slandered someone. And I wonder if you handle that."

"Yes, I've handled that. First let me ask you something. I don't necessarily want the name right now, but is it someone well known?"

"Yes, he owns a very popular restaurant. But look . . . I have to know . . . could you tell me how much you charge?"

"Well, it would be two hundred dollars an hour, Lieutenant."

"And is there some kind of limit?"

"I'm afraid it's impossible to say. I have no way of knowing how many hours it'll take."

The Lieutenant closed his eyes for a moment. "How much would it be up front?"

"Well, that would depend on a number of things. But I'd say it would run at least five thousand, possibly a lot more. You see, it's not as if you're doing the suing and we could work on a percentage of an award."

"I see. Well . . . let me call back."

"Sure. I imagine you have twenty days to answer the complaint. Well, I'm not pressing but if you want me to represent you—or any attorney—you obviously can't delay too long."

"I won't. Thank you."

He sat at the kitchen table his face in his hands. And after spending a fortune just to retain a goddam lawyer, what then? What then?

TWENTY-NINE

AT FIRST HE DIDN'T move to answer the phone. But when it went to the third ring and Ann wasn't answering either, he picked it up.

"Yes."

Colin Ryan sensed from just that one word that something might be wrong. He said, hesitantly, "Are you busy now?"

"No. No. This is fine."

But that something or other in the Lieutenant's voice was still there. "Look, let me call you later. I was just curious if you'd learned anything more about Moogie's suicide."

"No. I spoke to a guy I knew years ago, and that's it they say."

"I see."

There was a pause.

"Well, I'll be in touch," Ryan said.

Then out of the silence came, "Look, you're a good friend, and you ought to know. Don Reed is suing me. For slander."

"Oh Jesus."

"That nephew of his who hated him so much told him about me talking to him. And I'm sure he made up a lot more."

"I'll be damned."

Another pause. "Anyway, I wanted you to know."

"Do you have a lawyer?"

"No, not yet, I'm looking for one I can afford if there is such an animal."

"Hell, I wish I knew one I could recommend. I can ask around but they all probably charge a mint."

"I'll see, I'll get one. It'll be fine, it'll work out. As I say, I just wanted you to know."

"Lieutenant, is there anything I can do?"

"No, nothing. You just take care."

"Well, you too. And I'll stay in touch."

"You do that, my friend."

As Ryan set down the phone, he found himself impressed by the Lieutenant's determination. He's had a gun pulled on him, he's been attacked on the street, he's worried about his memory, he's going through all kinds of bullshit, and now this—this. And yet he sounded unfaltering.

He thought what a hell of a book this would make, if it worked out. Then he wondered, almost in disbelief, if it was that book that was really becoming most important to him.

* * *

But the Lieutenant wasn't thinking of his determination. He was thinking about how hurt and upset Ann was, and how she was an innocent in all this. And he was feeling real hatred—that nephew, that goddam nephew, had just used him, had suckered him to get back with his uncle.

He got up and went to the doorway of the bedroom, where Ann was putting something away in her closet. "Honey," he said, "it'll be okay."

"I hope. Look, I'm going down to Marsha's for a while. She just got her daughter's wedding pictures." She picked up her shoulder bag.

"It'll be okay. I'll do something."

"Whatever you say." She started to walk by him, and he stopped her and put his arms around her.

He said, "I hate it when I hurt you."

"Oh, Jack, I don't want you to be hurt."

When they moved apart, she said, "Do you want to go to the pool later?"

"I don't know. Maybe. I'll see."

When he was alone, he went through the phone book to see if he could find an address for Jeff Rollins. Then he remembered that it was in the legal papers. And what the hell was he going to do with it anyway? What he was really interested in was Mike Dalenski's present address that Ryan had gotten for him. He was curious to know how the guy had made such a leap forward in his life.

He was writing a note to leave for Ann when the phone rang.

"Dad, how are you?" Peter asked.

"Good." He was surprised to be hearing from him in the afternoon. "Okay. Good."

"You sure?"

"Of course." But he was suspicious now. He didn't like Peter's tone.

"There's nothing new?"

God, Ann had called him. But that was so unlike her!

"Peter," he said, "I'm being sued. You know it. I'm being sued."

After a brief silence: "Dad, I don't want you to be mad at her. She's sick over this. I mean worried about you, and who else is she going to call if not me? She did the right thing."

"I'm not mad at her." And he wasn't. How could he be?

"Now who is it? She didn't say."

"The fellow who owns Dockers. The restaurant. You know. Reed."

"Jesus. Do you have any kind of case against him? What did you say about him?"

"I just asked some questions about him. I don't have a case yet. Not yet."

"Not yet?"

"Not yet. No, not yet."

"Oh, Dad. Do you have a lawyer, do you know a lawyer?"

"I talked to one. He charges two arms and two legs. Do you know one, Peter?"

"I'll see, I'll talk around. But they all charge an arm and a leg. Listen, maybe you won't have to go to court. Maybe you could settle. Or apologize. Say you're wrong, you're sorry, you'll put an ad in the paper, anything."

The Lieutenant took a deep breath.

"Dad?"

"I'll see. I'll see."

But he had another problem now. He was feeling lightheaded all at once, as if all the blood were draining from his head. He bent forward and lowered his head a little. Slowly it began to pass.

"I'll see," he said again.

* * *

He was too preoccupied to give the usual cautionary look around before leaving the lobby. And the sight of his dented fender was more depressing than ever. But as he drove away he began to glance at his mirrors, as if he were becoming refueled.

He started to head for Dalenski's address but then realized he was much closer to Darla's, and turned in that direction; he felt drawn again just to sit there and stake the place out for a few minutes. He couldn't get her out of his head, couldn't stop trying to figure her out. All he knew was that she was screwing with his mind, and that he hated her.

There were no parking spots near her building. He had to drive several blocks around it because of one-way streets, and as he was making the third go-around a car coming the other way slowed up and stopped next to him. The window came down and Darla smiled and waved at him.

He lowered his window.

"Hi," she called. "What're you doing around here?"

"Just going somewhere."

"How are you?"

"Good." Horns had begun sounding behind both their cars.

"Hey," she said, "how about some coffee?"

"What?" Though he'd heard her.

"Coffee." She began to point. "Starbucks. Down the street. Meet you, okay?"

She was sitting by the big window when he walked in. She was wearing black slacks and a white blouse.

"I'm afraid I hijacked you," she said with a smile as he sat down. "But I was so surprised to see you and I hated to let you go. Let me get something for us both."

"No, let me."

"You sit right there. I'm the one forced you in here."

"You didn't force me."

"Oh ho."

She came back with two mochas, and protested when he went for his wallet.

"Please," she said. "No, seriously, please." And when he settled back, "How are you?"

"Good."

"I gave up the club, by the way. But I told you I was going to, didn't I? It wasn't worth it, even though the money was good. It was taking too much of my time, and anyway I really got to hate the place. Not so much that place but the whole bar scene. And I've got some great accounts just about lined up. Pray for me."

"You know I wish you well."

"I know you do." Her face grew serious. "I read about Moogie. Poor guy. You know, I would have bet a million dollars that he was one person who would never commit suicide."

"His ladyfriend," he said, looking at her, "doesn't believe for a minute that he did."

"Really? Oh, that makes it even worse, if that's possible."

"She says he was talking about them getting married."

"Really? Oh, God. You know that story got so very little play in the news?"

"I know. I didn't see anything on TV."

"There was something on one of the channels but not much. Well, it's really a pity. So what're you doing around here, if I may ask?"

"Just on my way to see a friend."

"And I've made you late?"

"No. It's fine."

"Well, if you're ever around here again just stop in. Or call to make sure I'm in."

"I will."

"You mean that?"

"I do."

Driving away a little later, he found himself hoping again that she had nothing to do with any of this.

* * *

He was more than curious, was really anxious now to see where Dalenski had lived before he moved into that mansion. His thoughts kept drifting back to Darla as he drove, until he came to the street—and then to the house. He could only stare at it in amazement. It was as much a mansion as the one Dalenski had just bought.

THIRTY

HE STARED AT THE house. How had Dalenski bought the new place? Did at least some of the money come from the heist? Or was it all legitimate money, say, from the sale of this house? Or the whole thing could be wrong, Darla might have passed on for fact what was actually just a rumor.

He drew up about a quarter mile away in front of a few shops, and decided to try the drugstore first. He walked up to a woman at the counter.

"I wonder if you could help me. Do you happen know anyone around here named Dalenski?"

"Dalenski? I'm afraid I don't, but I'm new here. Why don't you ask the pharmacist?"

In the rear of the store an elderly man in a white jacket looked up at him from behind the counter.

"Pardon me, I'm looking for Michael Dalenski. I know he lives somewhere around here but I've lost the address. Could you tell me where?"

The druggist looked him over suspiciously.

"I know they're somewhere on Carpenter Lane," the Lieutenant said. "And I know they're moving but I don't know if they've moved yet."

The druggist seemed to relax. "Yes, they're at fourteen-twelve. And no, they haven't moved yet. But they are moving. And it's a shame. Nice people. Very nice."

* * *

So what had he learned? Not much. Well, something. He had learned that Dalenski probably didn't need bad money to buy that new place. Of course that didn't necessarily mean anything. What damn crook couldn't find a use for bad money?

Meanwhile the clock on those twenty days was ticking. Ticking.

He reached into the glove compartment for the manila envelope he'd brought along thinking he might finally read all of those legal papers. He glanced at them, but he didn't really want to read them now any more than he had before. He started to shove them back in the envelope when he noticed Reed's address; it was his farm, not the condo. It was only a few miles from here.

He didn't know why he wanted to see it. He lost his way twice on the country roads, but soon the farm lay stretched before him: maybe about twenty acres behind a small stone wall. There was a large stucco house and a barn, with some rusty equipment on one side of it.

What could the guy have come up with in there? Or what—it was a dreadful thought—what if Reed was totally innocent? He tried to remember what had made him so sure that Reed had been mixed up in something shady, but he kept thinking about what possible reason Darla could have had to tell him about Dalenski's new house.

* * *

It was almost five o'clock when he pulled into a spot that gave him a good view of Darla's building. The clock was still ticking away, but he had the sense of it ticking a little slower here; at least he was doing something. But it was hard to hold onto this feeling as more than an hour passed.

The front door opened and closed several times, but he couldn't place any of the people who went in or out. Some of them probably had something to do with the insurance agency in there. After about an hour she came out. Followed by Quint.

The Lieutenant hadn't known he was in there.

The blue car they entered wasn't hers. He ducked down when the car passed him, and quickly started the motor. He followed them for about twenty minutes until they drove into the parking lot of an Italian restaurant, and went inside. The Lieutenant pulled into the next parking spot that opened up, and sat there watching the door, feeling hungry, fighting sleep. Then about an hour and a half later, in the dark, he saw them come out, at the same time as a group of other people. She got in the front seat of the car. And almost at the same time another figure separated itself from the group and climbed in back. It might have been a man but the Lieutenant couldn't be sure.

He followed the blue car for almost three-quarters of an hour, obviously somewhere out of the city. When it turned off a lonely road into a driveway, he pulled over to the side, far from the few streetlights here. The lights went on in what looked to be an isolated bungalow. Quint had apparently driven the third person home. But after ten minutes the blue car remained in the driveway.

He drove slowly past the driveway. A mailbox stood outside it. He drove a little distance, u-turned and came back. Inching up and lowering his window, he reached out, opened the box and felt around inside. Far back, his fingertips touched a flat paper. He pulled it out and squinted at it in his dashboard light. Just an ad. He turned it over.

It was addressed to Jeffrey Rollins.

The Lieutenant drove a few yards and stopped on the shoulder of the road with his lights off. His heart was thumping. What could they be talking about in that house? Who else could be in there? Could there be an open window anywhere . . . ?

He didn't see the glow of headlights come down the driveway until it was about halfway to the street. He crouched down in his seat as the car turned his way and passed him. He began following it, with his headlights off. When he turned them on he saw that the other car had speeded up, but then after several minutes its lights disappeared and he had no idea where it had gone—until he saw that it had taken a fast u-turn and was speeding toward him with its brights on. It was heading straight at him, the lights full on him, then swerved at almost the last second even as he cut onto the shoulder. He bounced along, struggling for control of the steering wheel, and when he got back on the road a swift glance in his rearview mirror revealed that the other car was u-turning again and speeding after him.

He pressed down on the gas, saw those lights coming at him, then turned left with screeching tires at a small intersection, then right at another, then at a third. He kept looking in the mirrors but there was nothing behind him. He made another turn, then another, and found himself on an expressway. For several miles he had no idea where he was, until he saw a sign that said Center City. Now he knew which direction to take.

He stopped about a mile from his apartment house. He didn't know if Darla or Quint had been able to see him in their headlights. If they did, they could be waiting for him. Once more he wished to hell he had a cell phone; why didn't he when just about everyone else in the world did? He sat trying to figure out what to do. Go to the police station? Yeah, loony Lehman. If he didn't go home—and he'd have to think of something to tell Ann—where could he spend the night? He thought of his old sergeant but he could just see him privately rolling his eyes too. His old friends—it struck him that he knew more dead than living people, and most of the living were in Florida. He thought of Colin Ryan but even though he knew it was foolish he didn't want to go to him in fear.

He slowed up as he approached his apartment house, then felt great relief when he saw a police car parked near the entrance. He pulled quickly into the lot, started to walk over to the car, then stopped when he saw two people coming toward him. Darla and Quint!

The cop got out.

"Officer," Darla said, "thank you so much for coming here. Thanks so much."

The officer asked the Lieutenant, "What's this all about?"

For a few seconds he couldn't think what to say. "I live here."

"I know that, I know that. Were you following this lady and gentleman?"

"No." But he suddenly remembered that the ad he'd pulled out of Rollins' mailbox was still in his car.

"That's not true, Mr. Lehman," Darla said, turning to him. "I saw you. We saw you. And we took your license number."

"That's right," Quint said.

"I can't believe you were stalking me," Darla said. "I don't know what else to call it. You followed me, then you sped away when we tried to catch up with you. Why?" She turned to the officer again. "This afternoon I had coffee with him. We met what I thought was accidentally. I've known him for a while, and when he asked me to have coffee I never thought anything about it."

"That's not true. I didn't ask her, she asked me!" But that sounded so stupid, so juvenile.

"Oh, Mr. Lehman. Please. Please. You asked me to have coffee with you and you know it and I did it. But I didn't know you were taking it . . . any other way." Again she looked at the officer. "You know he used to be a detective, a lieutenant," as if he couldn't speak for himself.

"That right?" the officer asked him.

"Yes. Westend. In charge of it." But his tongue felt thick.

"What's your name, sir?"

"Here." He was fumbling for his wallet as if he'd been caught at something on the street. The officer looked at his ID.

"Sorry about this, sir, but I've got to do this." He began to write.

"Officer, wait, please," Darla said. Then to the Lieutenant, "Mr. Lehman, I don't want to hurt you. You're a former officer, you're a married man, a grandfather, and I respect you for what you were. But I can't have this any more, it's got to stop. Do you understand?"

A couple of residents were standing and watching the scene.

"I just hope you've learned a lesson," Darla said. "Officer, I really don't want to press charges. I don't want to hurt him, he's hurt himself enough, and I feel he's learned his lesson."

The officer looked at her, then at the Lieutenant.

"I'd accept that, sir, if I were you," the officer said. "And call myself lucky."

Yes, the Lieutenant thought, the clever bitch has pounded in the last nail.

THIRTY-ONE

HE WALKED PAST THE little group gathered around the entrance. He didn't look at anyone, even when one of the men said, "Everything all right, Jack?"

He nodded and walked to the elevators. Only one lamp was lit in the apartment, and a look in the bedroom told him Ann was asleep. But she would know all about it soon enough, in the morning, when the phones started ringing.

"Is Jack all right? He looked so upset . . ."

"Honey, tell me, what happened to your husband . . ."

"Dear, I thought they were going to take him away. I mean, the police. . ."

He sat down in the living room He couldn't remember ever feeling such rage. Anger, yes, plenty of anger, but nothing like this. If he could kill that bitch, if he could just take that neck between his hands and crack it! And how clever of her. No matter how bad it had been for him before, it was far worse now. Whatever he accused her of, she would be the one that crazy old man had fallen in love with, had actually stalked, and now he was striking out at her in revenge.

Leaning his head back against the sofa, he tried closing his eyes but her face stayed there and he had to open them. Eventually without being aware that he was tired, he fell asleep sitting up, and at some time during the night stretched out on the sofa.

Ann was having breakfast when he looked in the kitchen. It was a little after ten. She didn't look at him as he stood there or as he walked to the refrigerator for orange juice. As he drank it standing by the sink she said evenly, and still not looking at him, "So what happened? Do you intend telling me?"

"Who called you?" He knew instantly it was a stupid question. He was so embarrassed and angry that it was the first thing he could think to say.

"Are you going to tell me?" Still quietly and without looking at him.

"If you'd look at me I will."

She looked at him. Her face was expressionless.

"I wasn't following a woman. It's not true, it's a lie."

"All right."

"I wasn't," he repeated. "I swear. I swear on Peter's life that I wasn't."

"All right." Her eyes suddenly glistened with tears.

"She lied. She's very clever and she lied. Stalking her! What a damn brain it takes to think of that! I was tailing a bunch of crooks and she was one of them."

She looked at him, her face expressionless again. "Do you want to tell me who she is?"

"Sure. Of course. Her name's Darla. She was involved in that gang we put away years ago. I'm sure she and a couple of the others are involved in this heist. And there's another guy. And this one's hard to believe. It's Don Reed's nephew, the guy who reported me to him."

She let out a soft breath, only to take in a long one. "Jack, what're we going to do about the case?"

"Get a lawyer."

She stroked her forehead with her fingers. "Oh, Jack, Jack, what am I going to do with you?"

He said, "Ann, just don't give up on me."

She looked at him. Her eyes were moist . He came over and hugged her and put his cheek against hers.

"Oh, Jack."

But it was more like a sob than anything else.

* * *

He didn't want to do it, but he knew he had to see Captain Hewitt again.

That cop last night had been from this police district, which could mean he'd either followed him for a while or had come directly here. Whatever, word that an old lieutenant of detectives was a stalker would find its way quickly to every cop's desk.

The captain was busy with someone and the Lieutenant had to wait about five minutes before he could go in. Captain Hewitt stood up from his desk and shook his hand.

"How's it going, Jack?"

"Oh great, great. You heard about last night, I guess."

The captain looked at him. "Yes. Of course."

"I want to tell you my side of it. And this is the truth."

He went into all of it that he could remember. The captain just kept looking at him. "Jack. You know this thing has gone all around. I mean, you being a cop. And I mean all around. And as far as Reed's concerned"—he lifted his palms—"I hear there's not a thing on him."

"Hewitt, he's the guy."

"Jack, look. Have it your way. I'm not going to fight with you. But if it wasn't anyone but a brother last night, that cop would have brought you in. You know that, don't you?"

"I know I told him the truth. And I'm telling you the truth."

"And if it wasn't for her dropping the complaint, you'd be in a real mess. Jack, I can only tell you as a brother and a friend, it's got to stop."

The Lieutenant stared at him. The son of a bitch hadn't heard a single word he had told him!

"Now it's the second time I've done this, Jack, but you know I called your wife about this. I know it's gotten you sore, but it's for your own sake."

THIRTY-TWO

SITTING IN HIS CAR, he felt swamped by rage at all of them—Darla, Rollins, the captain, the other cops, the stories spreading through the districts about him. And pressing against his chest was the lawsuit, that goddam lawsuit. He had absolutely no defense against it, none! And it would take away his savings, his pension—more!

He was trying to find that calm he'd always been able to find, but everything felt closed off to him. In the old days when he was stuck he had the Sarge to talk to, or any of the boys; he'd never been one of those commanders who looked on that as weakness. It never is as long as you use your own head. But now he couldn't even talk to the cops again, couldn't burden Ann anymore, was enough of a pain in the ass to Peter. The only one he could maybe air this out with, perhaps clear his head, was Ryan, though he couldn't get over feeling guilty about taking the guy away from his work.

He called him from the first pay phone he came to, though he had to look up his number in his notebook again.

"Ryan, this is Jack Lehman. I'd like to see you when it's convenient for you."

"Sure. Now's fine. Where are you?"

"I'm near Westend. The station house."

"How about coming over? Have you had lunch?"

"No."

"Well, we can have lunch here; I'll make some sandwiches. My girlfriend was supposed to come over but she can't make it, so if you don't mind being second . . ."

"I don't know about lunch, but I'll see you. Thanks."

Ryan opened his door almost the moment the Lieutenant buzzed, and held out his hand. "Glad you could make it."

Ryan asked him if he'd like something to drink, but the Lieutenant said no. His head felt so full. He wasn't even sure how much he'd already told him.

"I told you they took away my gun after that guy grabbed me, didn't I?"

"No. Not that part of it."

"Well, they took away my gun." But that's not what he wanted to tell him. "Anyway, about Darla. Last night I followed her and this guy Quint from her place—you know about Quint, don't you? Anyway, I followed them and you know who they met? Don Reed's nephew, Rollins. Ryan, they're all tied in on this."

"Holy hell!"

"But that's not all. They had dinner and then I followed them and they drove to Rollins' house. After they dropped him off they spotted me in my car on the road and they started chasing me. I lost them but when I got back to the apartment house there's this cop waiting for me. And she tells him I was stalking her. Stalking her."

"You've got to be kidding."

"I happened to have run into her in the afternoon and she said how about us going to Starbucks. And we did and we had a nice conversation. So she tells this cop I'd asked her to meet me there. It's like I'd been after her all along."

"What a bitch!"

"You won't believe this," he gave a bitter laugh, "but she said she wasn't going to press charges. She wasn't going to press charges, can you believe that? And everyone believes her, what a nice person. And I'm a stalker now. A seventy-three-year-old stalker."

"Let me get this straight. The cops believe her over you."

"Oh, yeah. The cops believe her over me. Those crooks got me now. I'm a perverted old stalker."

"She's one hell of a clever lady, isn't she?"

"Oh, is she." He found himself wanting to tell him how he could have put her away years ago, or at least tried to, but it was something he'd never told anyone. And maybe it was enough that he knew it himself.

"So where," Ryan asked, "do things stand now?"

"The damn lawsuit. That's never out of my head."

"Did you get a lawyer?"

"Not yet. But I will."

"And what's next on this?"

"I don't know, I'm not sure."

"Let me ask you, what do you know about this guy Rollins besides he's a prick?"

"All I know is he's apparently single, holds down a job, and is either trying to get back with his uncle or the whole thing was a set-up from the start."

"So except for Rollins, the whole gang you put away years ago is behind it."

The Lieutenant thought. "I don't know about that. I don't think Moogie was; in fact I'd bet anything against it. And then there's this Mike Dalenski. He's the only one I haven't seen Darla with. And did I tell you about his house? She told me that he just bought a mansion—like he came into big money. But I found out that his old house was already a mansion. So that's the second full-of-crap story she told me. And you know what that tells me?"

"He's not involved."

"Right. He ain't"—he used the word deliberately—"involved."

He wasn't aware until now of how clearly he'd begun thinking again, of how excitement was building in him once more. A little later, as they went on talking, it didn't seem like a bad idea after all when Ryan asked if he would like some lunch.

* * *

Colin Ryan walked down to the first floor with the Lieutenant and said goodbye to him on the sidewalk. He stood watching him walk to his car, this man who'd actually worried him when he first came in: he'd looked troubled and so old. But his handshake had become firm again and he was walking vigorously. Ryan had never thought of it this way before, but he realized now that the guy's enemies had become his enemies too.

THIRTY-THREE

THE LIEUTENANT DECIDED TO drive directly to Mike Dalenski's instead of calling first and giving him the opportunity to put him off. Only a couple of cars and a van were on his lot; all the limousines were out. The man behind the desk in the shack said, "What can I do for you?"

"I'd like to see Mike. Is he in?"

"He's in," with a motion of his head toward the closed office, "but he's busy right now."

"I'll wait."

"Can I tell him who's waiting?"

"Tell him Jack Lehman."

The man phoned and said it would be a while.

The Lieutenant took one of the only two chairs there. Another man came in, sat down and went in when Dalenski's door opened and someone came out. This happened again, but the Lieutenant intervened before it could happen a third time. He stood up quickly and went to the door just as it opened.

"Mike, can I see you? This is important."

Dalenski was sitting behind his desk. "Come in and close the door. Lehman, this is getting to be a pain in the ass." But he motioned him to a chair.

"Mike, I'm here because I trust you."

"You trust me?" He smiled. "Hey, it's my first merit badge."

"It's about you, Darla and something else."

"Well, the something else better be pretty interesting because there's nothing between Darla and me. Now what's the story?"

"It's mighty big. I'm sure she and Quint helped pull off a big haul, a huge haul."

Dalenski's eyes narrowed but he didn't say anything.

"A big haul," the Lieutenant repeated. "And Darla let me know that you just bought yourself a fine new home, in fact a mansion."

Dalenski's frown deepened. Then he stood up and exploded. "Why, that bitch, that little bastard! So I bought a new place. I've got a nice place, but I bought a new one. We'll be moving in."

"I know."

"You checked on me."

"I checked out her story, Mike."

"That bitch! I've got a wife, I've got two great kids, I want to give them everything. I'm doing good, thank God, and I've made great investments. And she tells you that shit!"

"You must have told her about the house."

"When? Let me think. Yeah. She calls me like a few days ago. Out of the blue. 'How are you, Mike, how's it going, what's new? I've been thinking about you.' Yeah, thinking about me. And I asked how she was doing and I told her about myself and I guess about the house."

"When did you talk to her before that?"

"I don't know, a year, two years. And she came on to me. Subtle but she came on, I wasn't born yesterday. But I hated her, and I don't know why I forgot how much I hated her. And there I am talking how are you and I'm fine and I bought a new house."

"Why'd you hate her?"

"I don't know if you remember this or not but she used to go out with my brother. Poor Emil. Poor guy. And I'm going to tell you something I never told before. She was shit-deep in what we pulled. But my brother protected her and he made sure that we protected her. 'Don't say a word against her!' And then what does she do? When he's in the can she doesn't even answer his letters. And then it's like I'm supposed to forget all that, and there she was talking about us getting together."

Every instinct told the Lieutenant the man was telling the truth, that he was one of those ex-cons he'd put away who changed, who you could trust with your family's lives after that. "Do you know Don Reed? From Dockers?"

"That bullshitter. I know him like everyone else knows him."

"You hear a lot of things, I'm sure. Ever hear anything about him losing a lot of money lately?"

"No. I hear a lot of things but I didn't hear—" He stopped. "You mean he's the one lost . . . ?"

"Well, let's just say his name came up."

"Can't help you there."

"What about his nephew, Jeff Rollins? Do you know him?"

"Oh, that guy. He used to be his maitre d' once in a while. I don't really know him but—you know, me and my competitors aren't exactly enemies. Competitors but not enemies. And we exchange stories. And one of them told me just last week that this guy hires a stretch to Atlantic City and back, and when my friend won't take a check, the guy keeps saying he has no money, he has no money, he lost it all. And then my friend gets out of the car and this guy's eyes get this big, and my friend follows him in the house and the bum goes somewhere in there and comes back with cash."

* * *

The Lieutentnat wondered as he drove to Jeff Rollins' house if he would have the guts to break in. Or if he was crazy enough. He'd done plenty of break-ins as a cop but always with a warrant. The only warrant he had now was in his head. He knew that somewhere in that house was Rollins' cut of the money. Or what was left of it.

But he also knew that a neighbor could spot him and he would be brought out, cameras whirring, his hands cuffed behind his back.

It took him less than half an hour to reach the road that led to the house, a road bordered by isolated farmhouses, but once on it he found himself caught in a line of cars. He was sure there was an accident ahead but after a few minutes he saw the first of several signs by the side of the road announcing a "July Fair." That explained the traffic and also reminded him that today was Saturday: all days felt alike since he'd retired. And here he'd counted on Rollins being at work in the city. Even if the guy wasn't here, even if there were no cars in the driveway, there'd be a million witnesses if he pulled in there.

The traffic seemed to be speeding up a little, stopped altogether and then began moving again. Now he could see an officer in the middle of the road directing traffic into the entrance to the fair or straight ahead. He picked up a little speed, found himself in heavy traffic again, probably people leaving the fair. He looked to his left, guessing that the house was one of those just ahead. He wondered if he would recognize it in daylight.

There it was. The bungalow.

As he came closer he saw something that sent a pounding against his ribs. Rollins was riding a power mower across the large lawn. And Darla was standing there watching him.

Quickly he turned his head to the side; with that traffic, he couldn't pick up speed. He tried to wish himself safely past the house but he could picture her running inside and calling the police. That stalker again!

There were only a couple of cars in front of him now, and then there were none as the road opened only to farmland. He slowed up at a roadsign, thinking it would direct him to the city but it gave the mileage to towns he knew only by name. Ahead of him was a red light at a quiet little intersection. He slowed and stopped.

He glanced automatically at his rearview mirror. A car was pulling up behind him. He glanced at it casually, then felt a hot rush of blood as he glimpsed a figure running toward him from the passenger side. His hand darted for the button to lock all the doors but instead hit one that opened a rear window. Then the door opened on the passenger side and Jeff Rollins slid in, pointing a revolver at him.

"Just drive slowly and carefully, old man."

THIRTY-FOUR

He came out of an instant's shock wanting to lunge at him. But the gun pressed against his side and the voice said, "Drive, drive, just drive, drive, old man, drive!" His hands tight on the wheel and his heart pumping, he found himself pulling slowly from the light. The voice said, "Faster goddam it, faster, not too fast, not too fast, there, keep it there." He fought to stay calm, trying to think where he could smash into a tree or go into a gully. Rollins said, "She's right in back of us, she's driving right in back of us, so do anything and you're dead as shit and we're out of here, hear me? You hear me? So do exactly what I say. Exactly."

He directed him to take roads that avoided the crowded road to the fair, and finally to a dirt lane that brought them to the rear of the cottage, where Rollins had him pull into a garage. Rollins slid across the front seat after him, prodded him out of the car and into the back door.

After a whispered discussion with Darla, Rollins pushed him into a chair in the kitchen, where she drew the blinds on the two windows. She didn't look at the Lieutenant. She was pale, agitated.

"You have rope?" she demanded.

"Rope? No, I don't have any rope."

"What do you mean you don't have any rope?"

"I don't, I don't have any rope."

"You have wire, you must have something!"

"I don't know, I don't think so."

"What do you mean you don't think so?"

"Hey, don't yell at me. Don't yell at me. Why would I have rope? I didn't even know what you were doing until you started yelling and running to the car."

"Look, just watch him, okay? Okay?"

She whirled and ran up the stairs in the living room, and came down holding some bed sheets.

"You got scissors?"

"Sure I got scissors."

"Where? Where?"

"That drawer. Over there. Not that one. That one. Yes."

The gun against the back of his head, the Lieutenant watched her cut some long strips from the sheet; she brought them over to Rollins. Then she held the gun while he followed her directions and tied the Lieutenant's wrists behind him and bound his ankles together. Rollins yanked hard at the knots.

"Now what," he wanted to know, "do we do about shutting him up?"

She opened the counter drawers and took out a dishcloth. Rollins stuffed it in the Lieutenant's mouth. Only then did she look him in the face.

"I never," her voice trembled, "wanted this shit to happen! But you wouldn't stop, goddam you, why didn't you stop, why didn't you stop?" Then she looked away quickly, to Rollins. "I'm calling Quinty."

"Why?" he demanded. "Why?"

"What do you mean why? We need him! What do you mean why?"

"We don't need him!"

"Don't be a damn ass!"

She went into the living room, Rollins trailing. The Lieutenant tried pushing his arms against the strips but felt that he was only tightening them. He tried again before letting his body go limp. He could hear her on the phone, but only barely. He was thinking mostly about just trying to breathe through the thick taste of the cloth in his mouth. And to avoid panic.

After about half an hour, the Lieutenant caught a glimpse of Quinty in the living room. His first words to Darla were furious: "What the hell are you doing here in the first place?"

"Don't give me that, buddy, I don't want to hear that, don't give me that!"

"I don't care what the hell you want to hear! What were you doing here?"

"Will you shut up?"

"I'm no goddam Reed, sister! I'm not one of your—your guys!"

"Look, you son of a bitch, don't talk to me like that! I'm not going to hear it, I'm not gonna listen!"

"You're gonna listen!"

"Get out of here!" She was screaming now. "Get out of here, you son of a bitch, get out!"

"I oughta get out, I oughta leave you here! And you, you son of a bitch," obviously turning on Rollins, "I ought to break every fucking bone—"

"Stop it!" she was shouting. "Stop it! Stop it! Stop it!"

"Don't tell me what to do, goddam you! Don't you tell me what to do!"

The Lieutenant, leaning forward in his chair, was hoping with beating pulses that they would kill each other, that he'd hear shots, furniture overturning, anything. In the old days, oh, he'd hold them in separate rooms like he'd done with so many bums, the smartest, the meanest—"He did this to you," "She did this to you," building them into a rage of fear and suspicion so they couldn't talk fast enough against each other. But the living room became quiet. Quint walked into the kitchen, his face red and ugly.

"You old son of a bitch!" He looked like he wanted to kick him. "You fucking no-good bastard!"

He stood there, breathing heavily. Then he reached over and yanked at the bindings. Darla and Rollins were standing in the entryway. "Watch him," he ordered Rollins.

Rollins remained standing there while the other two went back to the living room.

"Why didn't you stay the hell out of it?" he demanded furiously.

The Lieutenant looked away from him, trying to concentrate on breathing with this huge wad in his mouth.

"What'd you care if my fat-ass uncle lost money? You didn't see him yelling for the cops, did you? Did you? So goddam rich but all he wanted to do was keep more! More, more, more!"

The Lieutenant looked at him.

"'Hello, Mrs. Who-ha.'" Rollins gave a falsetto imitation of Reed's voice. "'And how are you, Senator? And how's that pretty wife of yours, doctor? And hello there, and how are you there?' Oh, that bullshitter! The king of bullshitters! But he's got it stuffed in his nose now! Can't even tell the cops."

"Jeff," Darla called out a warning from the living room, "shut it off."

"Oh, it's funny, funny, funny."

"That's enough, Jeff!"

Rollins peered over his shoulder into the living room. He moved angrily to a point in the archway where he could see both rooms. The Lieutenant told himself to keep concentrating on his breathing, try not to gag, try to stay calm. Try to think.

He felt so dumb, so stupid! And just look whose hands he had fallen into!

And he had only until dark. Of that he was sure.

* * *

For the next few hours Rollins and Quint took turns watching him. Darla came in only once, and went straight to the refrigerator without looking at him. He watched her take out a jug of water and fill a glass and throw her head back and drink it. He wondered if she would ask him if he wanted a drink but she didn't. It was as though he were dead already.

He leaned forward, just breathing, breathing. The taste of the cloth in his mouth made him feel sick He kept trying to think of a way out, to make some sense out of the whirl of thoughts bombarding his brain. He tried too to listen to what they were saying in the living room, as if he was still on duty and that would do any good.

But they kept their voices down most of the time. Darla and Quint seemed to be arguing; at one point she yelled, "If you don't stop I'm walking out, I don't care what happens I'm walking out." Quint shouted back, "Goddam it, go then, go!" But seconds later he was saying, "Hon-ey. Come on, hon-ey." Then the quiet talking began again. Once he thought he heard Quint say "Moogie" and his adrenaline surged, as though he could do anything about it.

* * *

It was getting dark. His arms ached; his legs felt stiff. But his mind never stopped racing: what if they did this or that? And would there be a split second or two when he could find some kind of opportunity? But he was just repeating every possible scenario over and over again. And trying not to think about Peter and Ann.

Rollins had been watching him for the past hour, and seemed to be growing edgier. He kept going to the refrigerator, peering outside through a corner of the window shades. Twice he came over and yanked at the binding though, like Darla, he didn't look at his face. Finally he walked to the archway. "For Christ's sake already." There was something about the way he said it that tightened the Lieutenant's heart.

No one answered.

"Hey, for Christ's sake."

The Lieutenant heard the scrape of a chair, and, his heart beating faster, he stared at them, trying to read their faces as the three of them came into the kitchen.

Only Quint met his eyes, and then just for a second. He bent over and loosened the strips, tossed them away, then grabbed him under the armpits and lifted him up.

The Lieutenant sagged heavily to the floor.

"Help me, for Christ's sake! Help me!" Rollins came over and the two of them lifted him up. They dragged him, feet sliding, out into the garage and shoved him into the back seat of his car. Rollins got in back with him, holding the gun while Quint slid in behind the wheel, a washcloth on each hand.

They drove off, with Darla following in her car.

The Lieutenant sat slumped forward, motionless—but his mind was still racing. After several miles they turned into a bumpy dirt road, slowed down and rolled to a quiet stop. He was yanked back into a sitting position. In that instant before the headlights went off and blackness closed in, he saw the wide shimmer of water. It was the river.

He let his head fall back limply.

"Come on, come on. Let's go." Quint climbed out and opened the back door, his hand covered by the washcloth. "Come on, you old son of a bitch. Come on." Quint seized him under the arms.

But he sagged as much as he could, forcing Quint to drag him across the seat and out of the car almost inch by inch. Once outside, he deliberately sank to the ground, the gun against his head.

"Get up, you old bastard!"

They dragged him down a low embankment, his knees hitting the ground, his feet sliding behind him. He could hear the splash of water in the blackness, but he made himself stay limp though everything in him was screaming to try to fight, to go out fighting. He was in the water now, it was around his chest, his legs. The press of the gun was suddenly gone but a hand was on the back of his head now, then another, pushing his face under. With a burst of strength that surprised them, he started swinging to each side with his elbows, tore free a little and then more, and began kicking away at the water. And away from frantic yelling and the wild flurry of hands.

THIRTY-FIVE

HE HAD TO WORK himself to the surface to draw a quick breath. He guessed that the river was at least four hundred yards wide. He swam frenziedly for a couple of minutes. Suddenly his left calf cramped and a blast of pain went through his leg. He clutched at it for a second, biting his lips and fighting against going under. The current began carrying him down the river through the moonless night.

He floated in searing pain, kicking with his good leg, swallowing water. His arms were starting to give out. Then he noticed that he was caught in a little whirlpool, but the cramp seemed to be easing up. He could take deep breaths again, but he still couldn't use his leg. For a few moments, having been whirled around, he wasn't sure which shore he'd come from. Both banks looked the same, dotted with tiny lights.

He began backstroking and kicking with his good leg. He had to rest every so often and to float. His calf was aching, and he had difficulty going into the crawl again, using only one leg. The cold was excruciating. He had no idea how long he had been swimming when with astonishment he felt his hands and knees touch bottom.

He stood up. Immediately his left leg buckled and he sank into the water again. He began crawling until he was on pebbly ground. For a few minutes he lay with his face on his arms, trying to gather strength. And savoring just being alive.

Finally he rose cautiously to his feet, testing the leg with some weight, and began limping through what he thought at first was a forest. But it was only a thin stand of trees that opened to a road. As he stood there trembling, an occasional car sped by. He waved at each one, his cold wet sleeve flapping around his arm, but only one car slowed down. It crawled past him, however, its three or four passengers staring at him. Watching it drive off, he had to sink down onto the shoulder of the road.

But those people must have called the police. About five minutes later a Lewinton Township police car pulled up, lights flashing, and an officer got out.

"What's wrong, mister?"

"Someone—people—" He was having trouble talking. "Tried kill me. In the water."

"What do you mean tried to kill you?"

"Drown me, tried drown me."

"Where was this?"

"Across . . ." He waved weakly.

"Across?"

"Other side. Across."

"Other side of the river?"

"Yes. Other side."

"Are you hurt?"

"My leg hurts. Got cramped swimming over."

"You swam the river?"

He nodded.

"Hold on, be right back." The officer strode to his car to call an ambulance. When he came back he said, "They'll be here any minute. Meanwhile, sir, can you give me your name?"

"Jack . . ." But he was so out of breath from trying to talk that he couldn't finish it.

"Can I look at your wallet?"

The Lieutenant nodded, motioning for him to take it from his back pocket. After looking at it the officer said with some surprise, "You're a cop?"

"Was. I was."

"I see, I see that. Do you know who tried to kill you?"

He nodded, but he was suddenly too exhausted to speak. He was shaking with cold, and he had the taste of river water in his mouth.

About fifteen minutes after the ambulance drew up, he was in a hospital emergency room. Later, as he was dozing on a cot under a heated blanket with an IV needle in his wrist, a township detective entered the room and came up to him. He introduced himself as Mack Whalen.

"How do you feel, buddy?"

"I'm here. I guess I'm okay."

"I hear you're a retired cop, Jack, a detective lieutenant. Sorry to meet you this way. Damn sorry. But you're alive and that's what counts. Now I hear from the officer that you know who tried to kill you. Who is it?"

"It's not one, there were three of them." Even as he said it he knew he was going to have trouble. "One was a woman, her name—" My God, her name, her name? "I'll think of it, it'll come to me, but there was a fellow named Quinn—I mean Quint. Quint."

"What's his first name?"

"I—I can't think of it right now. But the woman—it's Darla. Darla."

"Do you know her last name?"

"Yeah, but I just can't think of it right now."

"All right, just relax, try to take it easy. But let me ask you. You say there was a third person?"

"A guy, yes. But that guy I just can't think of his name right now."

"And you say they tried to drown you."

"Yes. But we were in this guy's house first. This guy, I can't think of his name."

"You have any idea where it is?"

"Mason Road?"

"There is a Mason Road. You know where on Mason?"

"Not right now, no. But I'll remember it all. I'm just having this goddam problem."

"I understand, Jack, and I'm sure it'll come to you. But see if you can tell me this. Do you have any idea why they tried to kill you?"

"Yeah, a long story. But honest I'm not with it right now. But there're some cops in the city who know about it. One's . . . one's . . ." There were several names but he was only trying to think of one. "Hewitt's one. Captain at Westend."

* * *

His wife and son were at the hospital within an hour. They kept asking him how he was, and he had to keep telling them he was fine, he wanted to go home.

"They want you to stay the night," Ann said. "We think you should."

"No, I'm not staying here, I'm going home."

"They think you shouldn't," Peter said. "You had bad cramping in your leg, you're under stress."

"My leg's okay and I'm getting out of here. I'll sign myself out. Did you bring my clothes?"

A couple of hours later he was walking slowly out to the car with them. His arms and legs still ached and he felt shaky. He sat in the front next to Peter. As they started off, Ann, in back, leaned forward.

"Jack, do you remember anything more about those people?"

"I will. Let me just get over this. Let me relax, it'll come to me. I must be in some kind of shock or something."

"Then you should have stayed in the hospital." Peter sounded irritated. "They didn't want you to go. They told you not to go."

"I'll be better off at home."

"I'll never know how you got away," Ann said. "And then swam that whole river."

He didn't answer; he didn't want to talk about it. But after a few moments he heard Peter say quietly, as though to himself, "Sure."

The Lieutenant turned to him, frowning. "What does that mean?"

"What does what mean? I was just thinking, I was talking to myself."

"You don't think . . . you don't think it happened that way?"

"Dad, did I say that? I never said that. I never said that."

"Pete, it happened like I said! I didn't jump in the goddam river because I like to swim!"

"God, no one's saying that, Dad. Come on. No one's saying that."

But Peter didn't look at him.

THIRTY-SIX

HE KNEW HE SHOULD have stayed in the hospital overnight. He still trembled occasionally, felt chills, and there was still the taste of the river in his mouth and the feel of water in his ears and his eyes burned. Worse than everything, he couldn't get his head to work right. But he hated hospitals; he couldn't stand the sounds and smell of them, and the helplessness.

When he got home he took a long hot shower, went right to bed and fell immediately into a deep sleep. He woke as he often did in the middle of the night, this time with his heart hammering as the dark water whirled and sucked at him. His panic gradually eased in his familiar surroundings with Ann asleep next to him. With this calm came Darla's face and with it—how could he ever have forgotten this? how?—her last name: McKenzie, and even Petrone. And then Quint's full name and—slower but it did come—Jeff Rollins.

He got out of bed quickly—too quickly, for every muscle hurt—and went into the kitchen, turned on the light and scrambled around in a drawer for a pen and a piece of paper. He printed the names carefully, and looked at the paper.

He had them!

* * *

In the morning, before breakfast, he called the township and was put through to Detective Whalen.

"This is Jack Lehman, the guy who gave you a hard time last night."

"You didn't give me any hard time, Jack. How are you?"

"Good. And my head's working again. I've got those three names and I've got their addresses. And I want to tell you exactly what happened."

"Terrific. Hold on a second. Okay, let's have them."

"One's Jeff Rollins. He's the one lives out your way." The Lieutenant read off his address. "The two from here are Darla McKenzie and Chris Quint." He gave their addresses too. "And this is exactly what happened."

After he heard his story, Whalen said, "You really went through hell, Jack. You're one lucky guy. And smart and in damn good shape. You feeling okay now?"

"A lot better. By the way, when can I get my car?" He'd learned that they had found it by the river.

"We'll be going over it. You probably can have it late today or tomorrow. But call first."

"Look, I'm telling you now, if you're looking for prints you're not going to find any good ones. Like I told you, one of them was holding some rags."

"Well, we've got the car so we'll see."

Although every muscle and joint seemed to have an ache of its own, he felt relaxed enough to have a good breakfast. But he felt edgy afterward; he wanted to hear something fast, though he knew it might take days. The call came the following morning.

"Jack. Jim Hewitt. How are you feeling?"

"Okay. Fine."

"That's good. Will you be home for a while? I'd like to see you."

"I'll be here."

"Well, I've got to go someplace and then I'll be over. Probably around eleven. All right?"

"That's fine."

Ann sat in on the conversation in the living room when Hewitt arrived.

"First," Hewitt said, "you look good. You really do. I'm glad you're all right . . . I just want to ask you some things, Jack, okay? First I want to get the story straight. So far I just got it secondhand. Now, this Darla and this Jeff Rollins hijacked you in your car and brought you to Rollins' house."

"That's right. But Darla was in her own car. It was Rollins pulled the gun on me and got in my car . . ."

"I see, and he made you drive to the house and they tied you up."

"That's right. In a chair, a kitchen chair."

"And what happened after that?"

"They called what's-his-name and he came over."

"Who was that, Jack?" Hewitt asked quietly.

The Lieutenant felt his face reddening. "What's his name, that guy . . ." And then with a soft release of breath, "Quint, they call him Quinty."

"And what happened then?"

"Nothing much. He looked me over, he went back in the living room."

"Wait, that's not all you told the township cop, Jack."

"What did I . . . ?" He was frowning. "Oh. You mean the fights. Quint had a fight with her, he started yelling at her about what she was doing there with Rollins. And it kept up, he was yelling at her and she was yelling at him. And he was yelling at Rollins too."

"All right. Then?"

"They drove me to the river. I guess Darla was in her own car. Rollins was with me in the back and Quint was driving."

"Were you still tied?"

"No, but Rollins had a gun on me."

"Go on."

"The two guys had hold of me and pulled me into the water and tried to drown me but I broke loose and was able to swim away . . ."

"Now let me get this straight, Jack. Don't get me wrong. It's just something I'm curious about and any defense attorney will have a lot of questions about. How does a guy—forgive me, but a guy in his seventies—who's held by two strong, much younger guys break away like that?"

"I can only say this. When they untied me from that chair, and I'd been tied there for hours, I didn't know if I even had the strength to stand up. And I told myself don't even try, let them drag you and carry you like you're a million years old. I didn't know if I would have the strength to break away but I was saving it for any damn second when I had the chance. I guess they didn't expect it. As far as swimming, I've been a swimmer all my life. All my life."

"All right. But why would they untie you and try to drown you instead of just dumping you in the river?"

"To make it look like a suicide. That's why they left my car by the river."

Hewitt looked at him for a long moment. "Jack, let me tell you their story as they tell it. First—and I'm just laying it all out, it isn't what we necessarily believe—this is a lady who called a cop because she claimed you'd been following her."

"A lie," the Lieutenant said calmly. "I've told you that."

"I know what you told me, but I'm just laying out their story, okay? Now, about yesterday. She and Rollins say they were alone in his house when you rang the bell and began yelling at her about reporting you to the police. They said they warned you they were going to call the police again, and you left."

"That's crazy! I was tied to a chair—a white chair—how would I know it's a white kitchen chair—"

"She said you did come into the house."

"Wait a minute. I came into the house and I was yelling? And she thought I was stalking her and they didn't call the cops?"

"Her story is she felt sorry for you. She said she knew you and you'd helped her once and she felt sorry for you."

"I see," he said, trying to control his temper, "and what about Quint?"

"He says he wasn't there. And those two say he wasn't there."

"You know, this is almost funny. They come a half-inch from killing me and it's almost funny. Well, of course it's all a goddam lie. And what about the river? What did I do, take a midnight swim?"

"I didn't say that, Jack. I just told you their story."

"Well, it's a goddam lie."

"Jack, I know your story. And I wanted you to know theirs. I owe that to you as cop to cop; that's why I came over. I wanted you to know exactly where it stands."

The Lieutenant looked at Ann and saw only dismay on her face. He said to Hewitt, "Wait, wait. Hold on. You're thinking maybe it's a possibility I made it all up, aren't you?"

"Jack, it's an investigation. I'm just telling you where it stands."

"But wait, wait. You people are thinking maybe it's possible, it just may be possible? What, that I tried to commit suicide but I changed my mind?"

"I didn't say that." Hewitt looked at Ann, as if for help.

"Or maybe—Oh, yeah. I was going to get them any way I could. So I pretended they tried to murder me . . ."

THIRTY-SEVEN

AFTER ANN WALKED HEWITT to the door, she came into the living room. "Jack, try not to be aggravated."

"No?" He looked at her from the sofa. "Why should I?"

"Just try not to."

"Right," he said. "Right."

"Look, it's not like he said he didn't believe you. He—"

"Are you kidding me? Am I hearing you right?"

She was flustered, "I said that wrong. I mean, you know, he's a policeman and he was just telling you they're looking at both sides."

"Ann"—he stood up—"I don't want to hear this. I don't want to hear about two sides. There's no two sides here. I don't want to hear about two sides."

"Jack, I'm only trying—"

"Look, the guy thinks I'm a nut case. Okay? He doesn't believe me. You were here, you heard. I can't spell it out any clearer."

She started to say something but he went into the bedroom, to the phone. When he came back a few minutes later he said evenly, "Look, I can pick up my car. Would you drive me up?"

"Of course."

They drove for several minutes without speaking. Then she said, looking straight ahead, her hands tight on the steering wheel, "Jack, I love you. Please let's not fight. Please . . . I almost lost you. I don't know what I would have done."

"Ann, I'm sitting here wondering if you believe me."

"Believe you?" She looked at him. "Of course I believe you. Why wouldn't I believe you? I was just trying to make that jackass sound better. I didn't want you to be so hurt."

He put his hand on her forearm.

"My fear all along has been that something would happen to you. And it almost did. I just thank God you're safe. We'll get through the lawsuit, we'll get through everything as long as we have each other. All I want is for us to live out our years in peace. That's all I ask, Jack."

He lifted her hand off the wheel just long enough to squeeze it hard.

* * *

Driving away from the township police headquarters, he was reliving in anger and frustration the meeting he'd just had with Detective Whalen. It had been like sitting with Hewitt again, only worse, because Whalen had said that Rollins was "a good guy as far as I know. A volunteer fireman up here . . ." And that Rollins was even willing to take a lie detector test.

Oh, yeah. The Lieutenant knew that trick. The other two would be willing too but of course their lawyers wouldn't let them. He could certainly ask to take one, but he'd seen too much in his day to put a lot of faith in lie detectors. With his luck it would turn out to be "inconclusive."

He was driving down a leafy road, with farmland all around it. He thought about Ann . . . But his thoughts drifted; he was back in that house trussed like a pig, and they were taunting him and—

His heart was pumping.

—and all the while the three of them fighting and—

"What the hell are you doing here?"

"Don't give me that, buddy, I don't want to hear that, don't give me that!"

"I'm no goddam Reed, sister! I'm not one of your guys!"

"Look, you son of a bitch! . . ."

He pressed his foot on the accelerator. He knew where he wanted to go.

* * *

There was only one car at the pumps at Quint's service station; both bays were empty. He parked his car by the side of the office. Quint was sitting at his desk, his back to him.

The Lieutenant stood quietly in the doorway. He wanted to pick up a crowbar and smash the bastard's head to a pulp. But he just stood there.

Quint looked up after several moments. Shock spread across his face but he quickly pulled himself together.

"Get the hell out of here."

"You want to call the cops? Call the cops. All I want is an application for a credit card."

"I'm telling you to get out of here."

The Lieutenant paused. "Oh, since you don't want to talk about credit cards, I might as well tell you. I want you to know, Quinty, I'm going to get you."

"Get out." His hands were on the arms of his chair.

"I'm going to get you. That's a promise. And that little shit Rollins? No problem there. He'll fold like paper. And Darla? Our dear friend Darla? Oh, we'll be working out a deal. I guarantee you."

Quint's hand reached out quickly and grabbed the phone. But he didn't lift it.

"I don't know what the hell you're talking about," he said. "You've been stalking her, you've been following her. You're crazy, old man, you know that?"

"But you know, it's not only me, Quinty. Jeff Rollins has been stalking her too. Only he didn't have to do any stalking."

Quint got up. "Get outta here or I'm gonna knock the shit out of you."

"Quinty," he said reprovingly. "Oh, Quinty. I'm not the one you should be thinking of knocking the shit out of. I never touched her. It took a lot of willpower though. She can come on mighty strong. Mighty strong. So when're you going to wise up, Quinty? She'll sell you out for a nickel—oh, maybe not for a nickel but if she wants something she gets it, you know that. She wanted Rollins, for instance, she got Rollins."

Quint stepped toward him, his fists clenched.

"Quinty, be smart for a change, cut yourself a deal. Do it first. Don't be second. Second, you know, is last."

"You trying to pull this shit on me? Don't try pulling it on me! You're last year! You're last century, old man!"

"Whatever you say."

"Now just get out." Quint grabbed him by the arm.

The Lieutenant looked at Quint's hand as though studying it, and then up at his face. "I don't advise this. I really don't."

His grip loosened.

"Before I go. Believe this or not. She's gonna screw you, Quinty. Like she's already screwed you. But that was just with another guy. And what's just another guy? Hell. But this'll be big time. I promise you."

He walked out to his car. Quint was standing in the doorway, staring at him.

* * *

Soon after he got home he called Colin Ryan. He didn't want him to hear the story on the news, if it played on the news at all, which it probably wouldn't as long as the cops had doubts about him. Ryan listened intently. "They don't believe you?"

"Ryan, why should they believe me? I'm senile, don't you know?"

"Oh yes, I forgot."

Ann had to make a call after that, and as soon as she hung up the phone rang. She took it, and said, "It's for you."

"Mr. Lehman," a young voice said, "this is Sally Martin. I'm Mrs. McKenzie's secretary. Darla McKenzie?"

"Yes." He felt a sudden heat rush through his chest.

"I just want to know if she called you."

"Today? No. Why?"

"She was trying to but she couldn't get through. Then she had to do something and she asked me to call. I just got home and I couldn't reach her and that's why I'm calling you to see if you heard from her."

"No, I didn't. Why don't you give me her number."

Most of his notebook had been washed out in the river. When he called, he got her answering machine.

"Darla, this is Jack Lehman. I'm home. Call me."

He stood for a while by the phone, as if that would make it ring sooner. He'd felt good after leaving Quint's, but then had to wonder what the hell he'd accomplished, what he could possibly do with Darla or Rollins. But this must have something to do with that—something! After half an hour he tried again. Instead of leaving a message, he hung up and went for his car keys.

"Jack, where're you going?"

"I'll be back soon. I have to see someone."

"Jack."

"There's nothing to worry about. I'll be back as soon as I can. If I'm going to be late I'll call."

When he got to her building he circled the block several times looking for a parking space. He was held up for a while by an accident to a bus. When he finally was able to turn into her street again, he saw flashing lights. An ambulance and police cars.

He double-parked quickly and ran over. Police were motioning back the growing crowd; people were staring out their windows. He heard someone say something about "shots" and then, from someone else, about a man running from the building. He watched now as the front door opened. They were easing a covered gurney down the steps, then rolling it to the ambulance. And though he tried to fight against it, he felt as if he were looking at someone he'd killed.

THIRTY-EIGHT

HE DROVE HOME IN TWILIGHT.

He wondered what she would have told him if she'd reached him. Would she have said I'm scared of this crazy and I want to tell the truth? Would she want to strike a deal? No, she would just tell more lies. Whatever it was, it would have been bullshit. So why, for God's sake, did he feel this stupid emptiness?

She tried to murder you, fellow!

No, not tried. Had murdered him. Only he got away.

He was eager to get home. But as the building loomed ahead, and he was about to turn into the parking lot, something struck him that he hadn't thought of at all. He'd been driving as if he were no longer in any danger. And it wasn't true. It was far from true.

He pulled to the curb.

He could picture Quint running from her place, frenzied, knowing it was all over for him, maybe wanting to get the man who goaded him into it. He began to drive slowly into the parking lot, and stopped on a slight rise that gave him a fairly good view of the three lines of cars. He saw no one. But Quint could be waiting in his car. He turned into a space, leaving the motor running, ready to pull out fast if anything unexpected happened. The front of the building was about twenty yards away.

He turned off the motor and got out, looking around. Then he began to stride quickly toward the building. The doors slid open and shut behind him. The man at the inside desk said good evening.

He walked to the elevators, still sure he was right about the way Quint's mind must be working. But he knew too that he had been putting himself in Quint's place.

* * *

The morning paper had pictures of Darla and Quint on the front page, under the headline SUSPECTED KILLER CAPTURED. Quint had been arrested without a struggle when a squad car officer spotted his license number. The story said, too, that Rollins was being held on "related charges."

The Lieutenant started getting calls during breakfast: the press, TV, Hewitt, Morrison. Hewitt called to ask him if there was anything else he could tell him about Don Reed—there wasn't—and ended the conversation with an almost reluctant, "Well . . . congratulations, Lieutenant."

Morrison was more than friendly. "I just want to tell you," he said, " I'm sorry I blew you off."

THIRTY-NINE

THE FIRST REPORTER to interview the Lieutenant was Bernie Taub, the *Journal's* crime reporter.

Taub was a short, solidly built man in his forties. After a fast handshake he said, "Hey, I hear that those two guys are just about doing handstands trying to blame each other."

"Quint and Rollins?"

"That's what I hear."

The Lieutenant was tempted to ask if Taub had heard anything about Don Reed, but it was as though he was still a cop. A good cop didn't let anything out until the time was right.

Taub held up a tape recorder. "You don't mind if I use this, do you? Okay, let me start off with the McKenzie woman. I understand you knew her years ago. Was she part of the gang you broke up?"

"Yes. She was part of it."

"I'm not clear on this. Was she charged with anything?"

"No," the Lieutenant said, shaking his head slowly. "No. She was never charged."

* * *

Reporters, photographers and cameramen filled his afternoon. Then about five o'clock he got another call from Bernie Taub.

"Lieutenant, I hate to bother you again but I'd appreciate any quotes you might have on this. First of all, I hear Quint's confessed to killing the lady. Went nuts because she was cheating on him. Did you see any signs of this, you know, when they had you?"

"Well, there was a lot of arguing. They weren't getting along at all. But I couldn't hear what they were saying most of the time."

"You have anything more to say on that?"

"No. What's there to say?"

"Now, there's something else. These guys are talking, and the word is they told the cops that a big robbery is involved in all this. Do you know anything about that?"

"Well, I do, a little, but you tell me first."

"Then you know about Don Reed?"

"I know about Reed. I first heard about him from that fellow I mentioned to you. Moogie."

"Well, Reed's denying all over the place that he was robbed. But what I hear is that Rollins suspected his uncle was stashing a lot of cash at his farm. He told McKenzie about it and introduced her to his uncle. And she apparently picked up enough bits and pieces to send Quint and this guy Joe Lippen searching the farm. And they found over seven hundred grand in an old ice house there."

And Lippen couldn't keep from boasting about it to Moogie.

"So from what I hear," Taub said, "Quint killed Lippen and this guy Moogie. And he's the one who came after you a couple times. So have you got any comment on that?"

"I guess I would just like to congratulate the police."

* * *

A little after six that evening he was in the kitchen when Ann called him into the living room. He stopped in the doorway stunned by the sight of his face full on the screen. The newscaster was repeating much of what the Lieutenant had already heard from Taub, but there was no mention of Don Reed. A few minutes later, the phone rang.

"Colin Ryan, Lieutenant. Hey, you look good on TV. Maybe they'll put you in a series."

"Yeah, I'm sure."

"Have you heard anything more about Reed?"

"Just that he's denying everything."

"Well, that's what he's doing. But I also hear that his lawyer is going to try to negotiate a deal. There's no question he was hiding skim money and trying to launder it. One way or another, he's in trouble. And that, my friend, takes care of your lawsuit."

Actually, he'd forgotten about it.

"So maybe one of these days we can sit down and talk about that book. I've been giving it a lot of thought. I see it starting with you going to the police with that story about Moogie."

* * *

The next day he got a call from a woman named Alice Valenki.

"How are you?" she asked.

"Good. You?" He had no idea who she was. A reporter?

"Just fine. First I want to congratulate you, but I don't even know where to begin. I just hope I have even half your ability and strength when I'm your age."

"Thanks." He couldn't even remember the name she had just given him.

"I mean that. Anyway, Lieutenant, you know we have your gun here"—oh, the detective!—"and I just want you to know one of us would be happy to run it over to you. You can pick it up, we can bring it over. Whichever you prefer."

He considered telling her to dispose of it. He hoped he would never need to touch it again. But even if it just stayed here in that filing cabinet . . . that little piece was so much a part of him.

"Yes, thanks a lot. I'd appreciate it if someone would bring it over."

* * *

That afternoon he and Ann went to the pool, he a little reluctantly as always: he loved to swim but the pool talk was not his talk; his world was not theirs.

After hellos all around, he relaxed on the lounge chair, thinking about Peter, who had just visited, and who wasn't talking about neurologists any more. He himself had brought it up: He was going to give it some thought. But he was no longer worried abut his condition. Whatever happened.

He got up shortly and dived into the deepest part of the pool. He stopped swimming after fifty laps and leaned back against the edge, stretching his legs. For the first time all his aches and pains had disappeared.

"Jack," a man called to him from a chair, "congratulations. When's your next case?"

The Lieutenant smiled back at him. Then he pushed away to swim a few more laps.